Boss

Game Changer series

Deborah Armstrong

Boss
By Deborah Armstrong
© Copyright 2020

ALL RIGHTS RESERVED

Published by

TERRAHILL PUBLISHING
ISBN trade paperback: 978-0-9950945-3-6
ISBN eBook: 978-0-9950945-2-9
ISBN audo: 978-0-9950945-4-3

Library of Congress Control Number: data on file
Cover, interior and eBook design:
Rebecca Finkel, F + P Graphic Design, FPGD.com
Book Consultant: Judith Briles, The Book Shepherd

First Edition
Printed in the United States

Prologue

Dane Andrews sat on his favorite stool in the Admiral's Eighth Bar and Grill watching the evening crowd acutely aware that whether through the scope of his rifle or his naked eye, he was always on the lookout for trouble. He'd picked this stool when he first entered this bar years ago when he was of legal drinking age. Dane liked how over the years the wood had been molded into a perfect seat for his size. He could sit in this stool for hours and watch every inch of the bar scene. Nothing and no one escaped his view. This stool was his spot, and his staff knew to keep it saved for him when he was in town.

He wasn't planning to visit his bar tonight. Business plans fell through and instead of heading back to his ranch, Dane and Bates, his right-hand man, decided to have a few drinks and relax. Bates sat beside him on his right. His attention focused on the woman sitting next to him. Wearing black jeans and T-shirt that showed off an array of navy tattoos on his muscled arms, Bates instantly attracted the woman's attention within minutes of her entering the bar. Dane smiled as he listened to the banter between the two. Bates wasn't one for talking, more the strong and silent type, uttering a few words when required. It didn't matter to the woman, as long as she had his attention. And she did, at least as much as Bates could give her. He always had Dane's six, his back, and that would never change.

Dane nursed his Chivas. The regulars knew him well enough to give him a perfunctory nod. The local women had learned to stay clear of Dane, giving him a wide berth after being told more than once that he wasn't interested. He always let them down politely, never telling them the reason why he didn't mess with women in his home town. He preferred to stay clear of romantic relationships and the ensuing complications. He couldn't afford to be tied to a woman unless it was by the hour, and even then it was rarely done on home turf.

He fit right in with the evening crowd wearing cowboy boots, jeans, and a cotton button shirt, although everything Dane wore advertised that he had money. His handmade cowboy boots were freshly polished. His jeans, though faded, were a designer label, and his shirt was custom-tailored. Only his wristwatch looked out of place. It was a gift from his paternal grandfather upon his graduation from the Naval Academy. It was the only piece of jewelry he wore.

Dane turned on his stool to face the bartender and pointed to his empty glass. "Refill, please, Tom."

"Sure thing, Boss."

Dane watched the amber liquid fill his glass with appreciation. There were few things he valued in life: expensive liquor, honesty, and a gun that shot straight.

"That's my man. He knows his whiskey." A woman's arms wrapped around Dane's neck as soft, warm lips caressed his ear. She whispered so only he could hear, "Help a girl out. Your name's Gary, and you're my boyfriend."

Dane was one for playing games, especially those meant for the bedroom. The scent of her perfume and the soft purr of her voice pulled Dane into the stranger's game, instantly causing him to ignore his rules. He took a long swallow of his whiskey while glancing at Bates and giving him a wink to let him know to stand down. He could manage this. Dane turned on his stool to face his new playmate. He smiled with appreciation at the breathtaking woman standing before him. Auburn hair fell in waves past her shoulders, emerald eyes, set in a perfect face of flawless alabaster skin, sparkled even in the dim light of the bar. A glance of her body which seemed to be poured into a tight green dress let him know that the rest of her was damned spectacular, too.

"Red, what took you so long?" He got to his feet. "I was beginning to wonder."

Her smile let him know he made the right play. "Gary, this is John from work. Remember? I told you about him."

Dane's tall frame towered over the man. "Glad to finally meet you, John," he said as he held out his hand to him.

The man shook Dane's hand. His face took on a pained expression with every shake from the vice-like grip.

"The way she talked about you, I have to admit that I thought you were a fantasy."

Dane squeezed John's hand harder. "I'm not a fantasy and don't make my girl one of yours. Got it, John?" Dane kept the pressure on while the man tried to pull his hand free from his grip. "Don't go after another man's woman."

John looked down at his aching hand and then at the woman. "Got it."

"Good. Then take a hike. My girl and I have a lot of catching up to do." Dane let go of the man's hand and watched as he turned and skulked away from them.

"Wow. How did you know?"

"That the guy's a creep?" Dane winked at the redhead. "I can think of only two reasons why a beautiful stranger would approach me in a bar—one, because she needs my help to get out of a sticky situation, or two, she's hitting on me and wants what's inside my wallet."

"Nothing else?" She allowed herself a long drink of the man standing before her. Ash brown hair styled short on the sides and long on top. He must have been at least six foot four, with a body that looked as though it was no stranger to working out at the gym or other places. His cotton shirt fit him perfectly, promising a muscled chest and abs underneath. And his jeans covered large thighs and—her eyes lingered a moment at the fullness of his crotch.

She felt his finger under her chin, guiding her gaze to his. "Red, you approached me from behind. I don't think there could have been another reason."

"My name's—"

He stopped her with a light kiss on her forehead as he pulled her against his chest and hugged her. "He's still watching us. The game's still on."

"What do you suggest we do?"

Dane liked the feel of her in his arms. Her height and her soft curves made her a perfect fit against his body. He hadn't been with anyone who fit as perfectly as this woman. It didn't take much thought for him to decide to play out this game as long as he could. Recognizing the song blaring from the speakers, he looked for an opening on the dance floor. "Dance," he answered as he took her hand in his and led her deep into the mass of people moving to the music. "You can dance, can't you?" He placed his right hand on her hip and began to move her along the dance floor with a slow two-step.

"Yes, I can." Her eyes opened wide. "And you can, too."

"Don't look so surprised. Isn't this part of your fantasy?" He smiled, seeing the deepening blush of embarrassment on her cheeks. "What exactly did you tell Johnny boy about your fantastic boyfriend?"

"You're a fireman. You specialize in wildfires. You've got two days' leave before you head out again."

Dane nodded his head. "Lucky for you Alberta's got a lot of wild-fires going on right now. So why did you have to make me up?"

Red looked away from him, focusing on the exit light across the room. She needed an exit plan just in case.

"Red, you can tell me anything. I promise what you tell me stays with me."

She turned her attention back to the man. His eyes were chocolate brown. She always thought blue eyes were sexy on a man, but these eyes made her want to get lost in him forever. His nose was slightly off-center, and his smile just a bit crooked. He'd probably been in a fight or two, most likely won them because of his build. A thin scar above his lip made her sure that this man could fight. With every moment studying him, she realized that her fantasy boyfriend would look exactly like him. Perfectly imperfect.

"We're both doctors at the hospital. We went on one date. I quickly realized he wasn't the one for me. He doesn't like rejection. I thought if I told him I had a boyfriend, he would lose interest."

"And?"

"It made things worse. John hates losing. He became even more interested, grilling me about my boyfriend. That's when I made up Gary, so incredibly perfect that he would have to back off."

"It didn't seem to work."

"No, it didn't."

"What made you decide to pick this place? And why pick me?"

Red looked up at him. Damn those eyes. They made her want to trust him, and believe that he could keep her safe.

"Tonight, he followed me from work. I told him I was meeting you, Gary, and John insisted on meeting you. He dared me to show him a boyfriend."

"So Johnny boy didn't believe you? It's good to know you aren't good at telling lies."

"I don't lie." She saw the arch of his eyebrow, showing his disbelief. "Okay. I only lie to creeps."

"Why did you bring the creep here?"

"I saw the bar's sign from the bus, and I thought it looked like a place Gary and I would meet. Because it's late, there was a good chance that I'd find a man that would fit Gary's description, and maybe he'd agree to help me out. As soon as I walked through the door, I saw you and the man sitting beside you. He was busy, and you weren't."

"And then you went for it."

"I had no choice. I hoped you'd play along with me."

"You didn't see my face."

"I didn't have to. I saw your shoulders, and you looked like you'd do."

"I'm not a pretty boy. My face isn't perfect."

"I'm not into pretty boys. It's what's in a man's heart that appeals to me."

Dane laughed.

"What's so funny?"

He gazed down at her and held her stare. "I've heard that one before."

"It's true."

Dane twirled Red for a couple of steps before bringing her back into his arms while continuing their dance.

"I can't thank you enough for helping me. I'd like to buy you a drink, or a few if you'd like."

"Thanks. It's not necessary. I can buy my own."

"I won't sleep with you as payment."

He laughed again. He'd lost count the number of times women had offered sex as payment for doing a job, as though sex was a valuable commodity. It wasn't. Not to him. Pretending to be Gary for the night became more appealing than he first thought.

"I'm not expecting you to. Look, your creeper is still here with a front-row seat to watch us. You've got me until you decide to leave."

"I can't ask you to do that. You probably have plans. Someone to go home to."

"The only plans I had were to have a few drinks with my buddy at the bar. As you witnessed for yourself, he's busy, so now I can have drinks with a beautiful woman who wants to pretend that I'm her boyfriend for the next few hours. I'd be a fool to say no."

Dane spotted an empty booth and directed her toward it. Catching the bartender's eye, he motioned for two drinks.

"I don't know your name. What should I call you?" she asked as she slid into the booth ahead of him.

"Gary suits me just fine, as Red does you. Any objections?"

"No." She smiled, pleased with her new name.

"Good. That's all we need to know. For now."

Chapter One

Dane Andrews heard the light rap on his office door.

"Come in." He looked up from his desk to see Val Williams, his housekeeper, peek around the door. "Is it that time already?"

"Yes. Bates is waiting in the car. Are you sure it's okay for me to leave you?"

Dane got to his feet and walked around his desk toward her. He beckoned her to come to him. As she did, he opened his arms to her and took her into a hug.

"You have to go, Val. It's time to make peace with your niece."

"I know. But—"

"No buts. She's reached out to you. Hear her out."

"What makes you such an expert on my family?" Val asked him as she pulled out of his embrace.

"The fact that I don't have one. I'd give anything to have someone to call family." He saw the twinkle in her eye. "Even though you, Bates and Lucky are as close to family as it gets."

He wrapped his arm around Val's waist and walked with her to the foyer of his house.

"Don't worry about me. I've got Lucky here to look after me. Besides, you're only away for a few hours. I think I can last that long."

"I know. But what if—"

"No what ifs. There's no point worrying about what you can't change. Lucky and I are going to watch the game this afternoon. We'll be in this room pigging out on snacks and beer, cheering for the Stampeders, and farting. Well, Lucky's the one that farts. Not me."

She relaxed against his side, letting out a sigh of acceptance. "Promise me you'll be safe. You know how I worry about you."

Dane helped Val with her coat. "I do, and I appreciate it. And you know I can't make a promise I can't keep. Now go. Kiss and make up with your niece."

"We'll be back for suppertime."

"I'm counting on it. You've got a pot roast in the slow cooker. I can smell it cooking from here."

As expected, Bates stood in the foyer waiting for her. He glanced at his watch to let her know that she had kept him waiting.

"The roads are clear. The sun is out, and there's no forecast for snow until later tonight. Let's make good use of what we've got."

Dane nodded his agreement.

Bates opened the front door and escorted Val to the waiting SUV. Dane didn't watch them drive off. Instead, he closed the front door then turned to face his furry companion.

"It's you and me, boy. What do you say we get some snacks before we watch the game?" Lucky's wagging tail showed his pleasure at the mention of snacks. "Let's see what Val left for us."

He spoke of Val with fondness. He knew that Val would make things right. Her family was too important to her to let ties remain broken for too long. He didn't know much about Val's niece. Val wasn't one to talk much about her past. Dane respected that, as she did the same about him. Val knew enough about him to allow her to work for him, and she knew enough not to talk about her boss to anyone.

They made their way through the spacious home to the large kitchen. It was a chef's dream with all of the gadgets and gizmos an avid cook or baker could desire. Dane didn't care about that as long as the person cooking for him did. All he insisted on was a bar fridge stocked with beer and one cupboard filled with snacks for both Lucky and him. Dane helped himself to a beer then opened the snack cupboard and perused its contents.

"What do you think? Pretzels for me and an elk antler for you?" He looked down at his dog. "No sharing. Got it? And try not to fart too much." Dane gathered their snacks then returned to his office.

He lived in a sprawling ranch bungalow on a fourteen hundred acre spread he had inherited from his grandfather. Twenty-five miles west of High River, the location made the place close enough to town for him to run his business without having to bring his business to his home.

He had to admit that his life had become a lot easier since Val entered it. When he hired her one year ago, she made it clear that the old rambling ranch bungalow needed redecorating. There was no sense having a housekeeper if there wasn't anything worth looking after. It didn't take much persuading to get Dane to agree with her. He had an immediate liking for the woman who was old enough to be his mother. She was tall and slender. Val kept her silver hair short above the collar. Her makeup was minimal, although she always had a lipstick tucked in a pocket. Her taste in clothing was comfortable chic—looking good in designer jeans and shirts.

She made his house a home with a professional's flair for decorating. She turned a dated bachelor pad into a home Dane was proud to own. It was still a man's home. However, the masculine tones were subtle, inviting. "You want to make sure a woman will feel welcome here, Boss. You don't want her to see you and your home as a fixer-upper project. That's the worst type of woman you could attract."

Every room in the house had large windows that offered a beautiful view: the foothills of Alberta, the distant Rockies, the vast pastures for grazing cattle, or the newly renovated outbuildings. His office looked out at the Rockies. It was Dane's favorite view because it reminded him of a night he spent with a woman he called Red.

He'd never stopped thinking of her. Once or twice, he thought about trying to find her. He always talked himself out of it. Their night together was perfect. At least it was for him. It was the only time he had broken his rules for playing games. Sometimes it was best to leave a perfect memory alone and leave it where it belonged, in the past.

Dane added another log to the fire burning in the stone fireplace. Taking the remote from the mantle, he pushed the buttons to turn on the football game. He was just in time for kickoff. He settled in his oversized leather sofa after placing his snacks on the end table. There was no coffee table in this room, nothing with sharp corners that could cause Dane harm. If he had a seizure in this room, the plush carpet would cushion him.

Lucky sat at Dane's feet working on his elk antler while Dane sipped his beer and munched on pretzels. He was used to his master yelling at the TV and ignored his curses when he hit the armrest of the sofa with his fist. It wasn't until the game's third quarter that Lucky turned his attention to Dane. He got to his feet and faced him, pawing at Dane's leg. At first, Dane didn't notice Lucky since he was concentrating on the game. It was the third down with a chance to tie the game. Lucky pawed at Dane's leg again, this time nudging him with his nose. That got his attention.

"You've got to be kidding me."

The timing of the seizure was maddening. Seven minutes left in the game and Dane was going to miss it. He pressed record on the remote, then got himself into position. They both knew what to do.

Dane lay on the floor and put a pillow under his head. Lucky immediately climbed onto his chest as though he were pinning him to the floor. His weight steadied Dane and calmed him when he came out of his seizure. Dane put his hand on Lucky's back.

"Good boy, Lucky."

Dane lay still and waited for the seizure to take him into the dark. Lucky's timing was usually spot on giving Dane a five-minute warning to place himself in a safe situation.

His seizure lasted for several minutes. Dane felt the reassuring pressure on his chest. His hands went to the soft fur and stroked it. He couldn't speak, but he could let Lucky know that he was coming back to him. A cold nose poked his face, followed by a lick or two over his mouth. Lucky did his best to look after Dane. They lay like this for a moment or two. His seizures had stayed the same for the last year. Dane found a small bit of comfort in that, although sometimes he was utterly exhausted afterward.

"Off," Dane said softly.

Lucky moved off of Dane's chest and lay down beside him. He waited patiently for his master to find his bearings.

"I'm okay, boy. Good job." His voice was barely audible, except to Lucky. "Damn. That was a good one," he said, still groggy as he got to his feet and stumbled onto the sofa.

Lucky sat facing Dane with his head resting on his master's lap. He kept watching over him while Dane fell into a deep sleep.

Chapter Two

Jules Montgomery heard the soft knock on the door of her hotel suite. "This is it," she said softly, knowing that she was out of range for little ears. "Don't screw it up, Jules." She glanced at the bedroom with its door slightly ajar and hoped that her daughter would nap for a little bit longer to give her some private time with her aunt.

She made her way to the door and opened it wide. There was no time to react, no time to think as her aunt took her in her arms and hugged her tight.

"I'm sorry," Val Williams said roughly, choking back her tears.

"No, I'm the one who has to apologize," Jules blinked away her tears. Now was not the time to cry. "I was in no position to tell you how to live your life." Jules sighed heavily before pulling away from her aunt's embrace. "Come in. We don't need to make a scene out here in the hallway."

Val nodded her head in agreement and followed Jules into her suite. She surveyed the large living room while she unbuttoned her winter coat and gave it her smile of approval.

"I heard these suites were quite luxurious. Now I can say I've been in one." She shrugged off her coat and draped it over the back of the sofa.

"It's a hotel room, Aunt Val. Nothing special."

Val turned and gave her niece a questioning look. "When did you become jaded? You act as though this is normal for you."

Jules gestured toward the armchairs separated by an ornately carved table laden with a silver tea set and sweets.

"If you'd been staying in suites like this for the last week or so, you might feel the same way."

Val took her seat and immediately began to pour the tea. She assumed Jules would expect it of her, as she did years ago when they would have afternoon tea. Jules joined her and watched as Val finished pouring then offered her a steaming cup of Earl Grey tea in a china teacup.

"I've been headhunted by a few of the specialty hospitals. High River General has offered me the position of Head of Pediatrics, and I've accepted."

"High River! You're coming home?"

"It's time, Aunt Val. I've been gone for too long. I want to be here with my family. With you."

"You had to go. I know that." Val took a sip of her tea. "Ned always said you'd go far in pediatrics. He dreamed that one day you might take over from him, as Chief of Staff. Maybe that will happen someday."

"Head of Pediatrics is enough for me. I want to have a life outside of the hospital."

Val straightened, her gaze focused on the wedding band that had never left her finger in forty years.

Jules cursed under her breath. "I wasn't referring to Uncle Ned. You and he had a wonderful life. He always looked forward to leaving the hospital and getting home to you. What I meant was that I want to have a life outside of the hospital for Becca's sake. I don't want her raised by a stranger, and I want her to know her family." Jules hadn't realized how much she missed her aunt until this very moment. "I'm sorry for the pain I caused you. I should never have said the things I did. Will you forgive me?"

Val placed her teacup and saucer on the table before taking Jules' hand in hers. "When Ned died, I felt utterly alone. You and Rebecca were in Toronto. I needed to make a change in my life."

"I asked you to move to Toronto. I couldn't understand why you would refuse."

"I belong out here with the mountains and the fresh air. I didn't want to move to a city I didn't know."

"I understand that now. Why else do you think I want to move back here?"

Val patted Jules' hand. "I made the right decision, Jules. I'm happier than I've been in a long time. You'll be happy, too. You and—"

"Mommy?"

Val turned her attention to the suite's bedroom door. "Oh, my. She looks like you did when you were a child."

"Come here, Becca. Come meet your Auntie Val," Jules said sweetly, opening her arms to her daughter.

The redheaded toddler ran to her mother's side and peered up at Val with bright green eyes. "Hi!"

"Well, hi to you, too."

"I'm almost five," Becca told Val happily as she held up five fingers to Val's face.

"I know. I remember when you were born." Val glanced toward Jules. "You were quite a surprise."

"Mommy says I was a gift."

Jules cleared her throat. "Would you like a cookie, sweetie? There's an oatmeal raisin cookie just for you."

"Yummy," the little girl cheered as she took the offered cookie.

"Sit with me while you eat it." Val lifted her and placed Becca beside her on the ample cushion. She watched the toddler as she nibbled at her cookie in a clockwise direction. "Does she always eat like that?"

Jules chuckled. "Only her cookies. Everything else she eats normally. I don't know why she insists on eating around the outside like that."

"Genetics?" Val mused.

"Not mine," Jules answered with a touch of sadness as she turned her gaze to the window.

"I'm sorry. I wasn't thinking."

Jules turned her attention back to Val and smiled. "Never mind. It's okay."

"No, it's not. How this little one came into existence is not for me to question."

"Little ears," Jules warned Val with a hushed voice.

"I have little ears!" Rebecca announced as she pulled her hair back from her face. "See?"

Val smiled. "They are perfect. Just your size."

Jules' cell phone buzzed. She got to her feet and walked over to the desk where she had left the phone. "I have to take this," she said to Val while she checked the caller display.

"Go ahead. Becca and I will get to know each other."

Jules entered the bedroom and closed the door behind her.

Becca smiled up at Val. "Mommy says you're going to live with us."

Val's eyes opened wide. "She did? Where are we going to live?"

"In a house. And I get to have a puppy. And you can look after me."

"Is that so?"

"Uh-huh," Becca answered, nodding her head in agreement.

Val turned her attention to the bedroom door. She and Jules needed to talk now more than ever.

Jules exited the bedroom at a quick pace. "They want me at the hospital. Now."

"We need to talk, Jules."

"Can it wait? I have to go."

"What about Becca?"

"Would you mind?"

"Mind what?"

"Will you stay and look after her for me? I don't know how long I'll be."

"I can't stay here. I'm needed back at the ranch."

"This is an emergency, Aunt Val."

"But it's not mine."

Jules stopped and stared at her aunt in disbelief. "Oh my god. Now is not the time to throw my words back in my face! I'm sorry I ever said that to you."

"I'm not throwing them back at you, Jules. I'm simply stating a fact. I have responsibilities to another person. I can't stay here and abandon him."

"You're not abandoning him. You're looking after your grandniece!"

"No. I'm sorry. I can't stay." Val stood up and retrieved her coat and purse.

"Then take Becca with you. Please, Aunt Val. Take her with you, and I'll get her when I can. I won't ask you to look after her ever again."

Val gazed down at the little girl looking up at her with hopeful eyes. She inhaled deeply and let out a long sigh. "She's got your eyes. I could never say no to them over twenty-five years ago, and I can't say no to them now."

"Thank you!" Jules said as she hugged her aunt. "I'll pack a bag for her with a few of her toys and a change of clothes just in case."

"Am I going with you?" Becca asked excitedly.

"Yes, sweetheart. Auntie Val's taking you to my place."

Bates stood beside the large black SUV waiting for Val.

She could see his imposing figure through the glass of the hotel's lobby doors. In the year that she'd known him, she had rarely seen him crack a smile. Maybe he would smile for Becca. She hoped his size wouldn't scare the young girl. The lobby doors slid open, and she stepped outside.

Bates glanced down at the little girl accompanying Val. "You have a child with you."

"Showing off your Commando training again?" Val teased, feeling nervous as she handed Becca's backpack to Bates.

"You're big," Becca chimed in as she looked up at him. "Are you a giant?"

"No, I'm not," Bates answered, looking down at her. "You're small." He turned his attention back to Val. "It's Special Elite, not Commando. Did you clear it with Boss?"

"No. Is there a problem?"

"There could be. How long is the child staying?" Bates asked while opening the rear door for Val and her charge.

Becca scrambled onto the leather seat while Val paused to answer Bates. "I don't know. Maybe overnight. Her mother will pick her up when she's finished at the hospital."

"At the ranch?"

"Yes. At the ranch. What's with the questions?"

Bates shook his head slowly. "Nothing." He gestured for Val to get into the car.

Val took her seat then made sure to fasten Becca's seatbelt before she did her own. Once Bates got behind the wheel, she looked at his reflection in the rearview mirror. He caught her gaze and held it.

"Does your niece know where you're taking her daughter?"

"Nothing's going to happen, Bates. She's a child, for Pete's sake!"

"I'm almost five!" Becca said happily.

"You want to see her after tomorrow?"

Val took in a sharp breath. What had she done?

Chapter Three

DANE HEARD the soft voice of a child. Her voice was steady, almost soothing. He concentrated on her words, trying to figure out what she was saying.

"Grandma, what big eyes you have. All the better to see you with, my dear. . ."

He knew that story from his childhood. Was he dreaming? It couldn't be a dream. This one was happy, pleasant, not like the nightmares that sometimes haunted him reminding him of the evil in the world. The children in his dreams never recited fairy tales. If he were dreaming this, he'd have to tell Doc that his seizures were messing with his brain now. He kept listening. He heard the pages of the book turn and knew that this was real.

Dane forced himself to open his eyes. He got his bearings. On the sofa. TV on. He held out his hand. Lucky.

The child's voice continued. "Grandma, what big teeth you have."

Turning his head toward the voice, Dane saw the top of a child's head covered with thick, shiny red hair. He reached for her, touching her ever so gently.

The reading stopped, and the head turned to face him. Bright green eyes set in a cherub's perfect face blinked at him. If he had been the wolf in the story, he knew this child would have slain him easily with her smile.

"Hello," he said hoarsely. He coughed to clear his throat.

"Hi."

"What's your name?"

"Becca. I'm almost five years old."

"Hi, Becca. My name's Dane."

"What's the doggie's name?"

"His name is Lucky."

"I like Lucky. I'm reading him a story."

"I heard that. You read very well for four years old."

"I'm almost five."

"Right. For almost five."

"I know lots of words. Mommy taught me to read. Does Lucky know how to read?"

Dane smiled. "No, Lucky can't read, although he knows lots of words."

"Like red and wolf?"

"No. Words that tell him to do things like sit, stay, come, and off."

"Off?"

"When he's on top of me, and I need him to get off me, I say 'off,' and he obeys."

"Oh. Okay."

"Who brought you here?"

"Auntie Val."

"Auntie Val?"

"Mommy had to go to work, so Auntie Val brought me here."

"Okay." Dane groaned as he struggled to get to his feet.

"You have little ears."

"I do?" Dane asked with amusement. "No one's ever told me that."

"Yep. And you snore."

"Do I? No one has ever told me that either."

"Are you sick?"

"No. Only tired." Dane ran his hand through his short hair, then adjusted his shirt and pants. "Why don't we go find Auntie Val?"

"Okay."

Becca got to her feet, clutching her book and a stuffed bunny. She held the book out to Dane. He took the offering.

Becca took hold of Dane's free hand and said, "I'll take you and Lucky to her."

The sight of Dane walking into the kitchen with her grandniece, hand in hand, made her cry out, "Oh my." Val rushed to them. "Becca, you were supposed to be watching your movie! I'm sorry, Boss, I got busy with making supper." Val bent over the child, "Sweetheart, you mustn't bother Mr. Andrews."

"He was sleeping."

Val looked up at Dane. "Are you okay?"

"I'm fine. We'll talk later about leaving children unattended." His piercing gaze made it clear that they would talk. Dane took a seat at the kitchen table and placed Becca on the chair next to his. "So tell me about your visit with your niece."

"Jules is the new Head of Pediatrics at High River General. She got called back to the hospital for an emergency. There was no one to look after Becca, and I didn't think you'd mind if I brought her home with me. Jules will call me when she's finished. She can drive out to the ranch, or we can take Becca back to the hotel. It's up to you."

Dane pointed to the window. "Have you looked outside, Val? No one's going anywhere tonight. It looks like we have ourselves a houseguest."

"Oh my," Val said as she witnessed the blizzard outside.

"Call your niece and let her know Becca is fine. There's no need for her to attempt the trip out here. We'll work something out tomorrow." Dane gazed down at the redheaded cherub hugging her bunny. "So, Becca, do you think Auntie Val will let us have a cookie before supper?"

"Is now a good time to talk?" Val asked Dane when she brought him a mug of hot coffee with a plate of cookies.

Becca was sound asleep in Val's bedroom, and Dane had gone to his office to finish watching the football game while checking his emails.

Dane gestured to one of the chairs in front of his desk. "Have a seat, Val." He closed his laptop and leaned back in his leather chair once he snatched a cookie from the plate.

"So, I take it you reconciled with your niece since she let you leave with her daughter." He popped the cookie into his mouth.

Val frowned. "Barely. I was no more than five minutes with her before she got an emergency call from the hospital. I told you that she'd been hired on as the new Head of Pediatrics?"

"Yes, you did. You must be very proud."

"I am. Anyway, what I want to say is that Jules got called back to the hospital and she had no one to look after Becca. She put me in a difficult position. I knew that I had to get back to the ranch. Bringing Becca with me was the only option."

"You could have stayed. I would have understood, and it would have been better for both of you."

"I never thought that it would be a problem."

"I know, but it could be. You haven't told Jules about me. Have you?" It was more of a statement than a question. Dane knew that Val hadn't told her niece about her employer.

"No! There wasn't much I could say to her in five minutes. Besides, it's only for tonight, and nothing is going on here that would make it unsafe. Your home is the safest place Becca could be. I wouldn't have brought her here if I thought otherwise." Her gaze searched his face for understanding.

Dane steepled his fingers across his chest. "How do you think your niece will react when she comes here to pick up Becca? I'm sure she's going to ask questions about me and this place."

"I don't have to tell her the truth."

"Yes, you do. You aren't one to tell lies, and I don't expect you to lie now."

"You're not a bad man, Boss. She'll see that right away."

"Not everyone has the same viewpoint as you, Val. Guns and guns for hire seem criminal to most people."

"The work you do is for good. Don't let anyone make you think otherwise." Her brow furrowed as she took in the haggard look on his face. "Was it a rough one today? You look exhausted."

He shrugged, allowing her to change the subject. "Nothing more than usual. I think it's playing with Becca that's tired me out."

"You didn't have to."

"I wanted to. Besides, I liked reading Red Riding Hood. Over and over again."

Val got to her feet. "She does like that story. I'm going to check on her then go to bed. Do you need anything?"

"No, I'm fine. Good night, Val."

"Good night. And please don't worry about Jules. I'll have a word with her."

Dane turned his attention back to his laptop. He opened it and clicked on the encrypted government file he had been reading before Val interrupted him. Another request to liberate a village in a war-torn territory in Central Africa, rescuing women and children held captive before getting sold into slavery, and young boys destined for the guerilla army. It was a never-ending occurrence. No matter how many times Dane and his men came to the rescue, another village would fall.

There were times when Dane wondered if it was worth it—risking his men to save strangers, especially when he knew what they did was only a drop in the bucket. There was evil everywhere, and they were a small group of men who could do only so much. Then Dane would open his desk drawer and pull out the file he kept, one filled with pictures of the many smiling faces of the villagers they had freed, and he would know that it was worth it.

He closed the file and shut down his laptop, locking it away in his top desk drawer. His bed called to him. He was tired, and he longed to fall into a dream-filled sleep.

She came to him in his dreams. The woman he knew as Red. She was perfection on two legs. The most beautiful red hair he had ever seen fell in thick waves to her shoulders. Emerald eyes that seemed to see deep into his soul sparkled with the promise of endless pleasure. In his dreams, Red always wore the same green dress that hugged every curve on her body. They danced, their bodies a perfect fit as he held her close. Her chin touched his shoulder, and she whispered in his ear for him to hold her tighter, to never let her go. All he wanted to do was to dance with her, hold her in his arms, and feel the gentle caress of her lips on his ear and neck. She had the softest and sweetest kiss he had ever known. She kissed him on the mouth. It was a warm kiss, wet and urgent. His dream moved them to his bed. Red now lay on top of him. Her weight pressed him to the mattress. He reached out to her, his fingers searching for the soft wavy tresses he remembered so well. Instead, he found short, cropped hair. And her breath was no longer sweet. It was warm and smelled of dog. Lucky.

Dane opened his eyes to find his eighty-five pound Rhodesian Ridgeback sprawled across his body, his nose to Dane's. Lucky's wagging tail let Dane know that it was time to get up.

"Good morning, boy," Dane said as he patted his dog. "Not quite the kiss I was dreaming of."

He rubbed the dog's ears and stared up at the ceiling, wondering about the woman he knew only as Red. He met her once when she approached him in his bar, looking for a man to help her out of a bad situation. He remembered how she wrapped her arms around his neck from behind and whispered in his ear, "Help a girl out. Your name is Gary, and you're my boyfriend."

There was no hesitation in jumping to the rescue. He could never refuse a woman in need. He played the role of her boyfriend perfectly. Happy to be Gary, her fantasy boyfriend. It was all a game. They didn't know each other's name. They made up stories about themselves, danced, drank, and fooled themselves into thinking there would be no strings attached. Red left his bed in the morning with her name invisibly tattooed on his heart.

Chapter Four

JULES SAT COMFORTABLY in the passenger seat of Dr. Mark Blackwell's Hybrid Land Rover SUV, thankful that the snowstorm from last night had ended and that the recently cleared roads allowed them to drive out to the ranch. She loved the rugged Albertan countryside in the summer, although the dangerous and often impassable country roads in winter made her wonder why she ever lived and worked in High River. She had to admit that living close to Uncle Ned and Aunt Val had a lot to do with her starting her medical career in her home town. Her stint in Toronto had converted her from country doctor to a prominent city specialist. The city of Calgary was more to her liking now, and since High River was part of the Calgary network, returning to High River General was the perfect choice for Jules.

The drive through High River brought back memories of a life she thought she'd left behind. She made sure they drove past the hospital. She thought of Uncle Ned and regretted that she hadn't been with him when he passed away two years ago. He'd had a fall. Val pleaded with Jules to come home to visit with her uncle. Val was sure that seeing Jules and Becca would help in his recovery.

"I can't," Jules told her. "He'll be fine."

"It's an emergency. Can't you see that?" Val cried on the phone.

"I have emergencies here, Aunt Val. I can't get away. I'm sorry."

Two weeks later, Ned was gone. His stroke had been fast, taking him away without causing him to suffer. Aunt Val suffered, and although she had never said the words to her face, Jules knew that her aunt hadn't forgiven her for not seeing Ned one last time. And Jules had regretted that she had not come when asked.

Jules tried to get her to move to Toronto, knowing full well that her aunt wouldn't leave her home and the town she had grown to love. That is why Jules found it incredible if not insane when Aunt Val told her that she was selling her house and moving in with a stranger to become his housekeeper.

"Aunt Val, why are you doing this? You don't need the money, do you?"

"Of course not. That's not the reason. I'm tired of living on my own. I've been looking after our bungalow for most of my life. Why not keep house for someone else? I can cook and clean to my heart's content. And the view, Jules—you've never seen the mountains like this. This place is heaven on earth."

"You don't know this man, Aunt Val. He could be a pervert. Maybe he wants to make you his sex slave. You're making a huge mistake."

"Well then, I'm making a mistake. I'm an adult, Jules. I've made my decision, and I won't let you ruin it for me."

Their conversation ended with tears and hurt feelings. Val put all of her energy into her new job, while Jules kept busy with her practice and Becca. Phone calls became few and far between until a birthday card to Becca was the last Jules heard from her aunt.

"A penny for your thoughts, or is that not enough for the new Head of Pediatrics?"

Jules blinked and turned her attention to Mark. "Sorry, I was thinking back to a time long ago."

"Was it a good time or bad?"

"It was good until I messed it up."

"Do you want to talk about it?"

Jules shook her head. "No, thanks. It's something I have to deal with by myself. A bridge that needs mending."

"Ah," he nodded. "Your aunt. Unresolved issues."

She frowned. "Don't analyze me, Dr. Blackwell. I'm not one of your patients."

His brow furrowed. "I don't need to be a doctor to know that you have issues with your aunt. She's the only family you have here."

Jules reached for his free hand and squeezed it. "I'm sorry, Mark. You're right. It is my aunt. It's just that I don't want to talk about her."

She didn't like to talk about many things. Jules didn't talk about her past, only offering a quick story to satisfy one's curiosity—orphaned when a teenager and raised by her childless aunt and uncle, then decided to take up medicine because of them. She didn't talk about Becca's father, relieved that single motherhood had become an accepted norm with no questions asked.

Jules turned her attention back to the passing scenery. Snow. Open space. Mountains. All seemingly held captive by a wire fence that ran parallel to the road. She kept her focus on the mountains and wondered if Becca's father ever looked at them and thought of her. It seemed like a lifetime ago when they took in the view of the mountains from his penthouse suite, and then made love as though there would be no tomorrow.

"You don't know who your aunt works for?"

"No. Aunt Val has never mentioned his name."

"Never?"

"She refers to him as Boss, nothing else. It sounds weird. I hope I'll be able to meet him. I'd feel better knowing who this man is."

Mark glanced at the GPS. "His place is coming up. Look out for a driveway on your side."

They hadn't seen a building for miles. Whoever Aunt Val worked for, it was apparent that he didn't have neighbors. Maybe he didn't want them either. They were indeed out in the middle of nowhere, Alberta. Jules wondered what Val thought about it.

"There," she said as she pointed to a gate coming into view. "That's probably the place."

As they neared the entrance, Jules realized that this boss of Val's had a thing for security. A massive gate built out of stone and carved timber framed the steel gate barricading the driveway. There was no sign on the entrance or logo to identify the place. Mark stopped the car and lowered the driver's side window and reached for the intercom button. As he did so, Jules noticed a security camera aimed at them.

"Smile," she said while making a thin smile.

"Jules Montgomery to see Val Williams," he shouted into the speaker.

Within seconds the gates opened wide to allow them entry. Mark drove the vehicle forward slowly as both of them took in their surroundings. He glanced at his rearview mirror and saw the gates close behind them. "We're in here for good," he teased. "No escaping now."

Jules gave a weak chuckle. "Don't say that."

"Everything will be fine."

"Of course, it will."

They traveled for a half mile on a driveway cleared of snow from the previous night's storm. Snow drifts at least six feet high made a natural wall along the way.

She felt the hairs on the back of her neck stand up. "This is creepy."

When the driveway ended, the enormity of the compound became apparent. There were two large barns, and at least six or seven outbuildings. All of them matched with white sides and green roof and trim. Across the driveway from them stood the residence—a sprawling log house with a wrap-around veranda.

"Damn. This place is—"

"A commune," Jules finished for him. "My aunt's joined a bloody cult."

"I was going to say impressive. Let's not jump to conclusions, Jules."

She took in the view. Even with three feet of snow on the ground, the place was immaculate. The driveway was cleared up to and around the outbuildings. Not a flake of snow remained on the cleared stone walkway leading to the house.

"I'm sure this place is legit," Mark offered as if to convince himself more so than Jules.

"Do you know of anyone who lives in the area who has a place like this?"

"No, but that doesn't mean anything. Val's employer could be a cattle baron or a dot com millionaire." Mark stopped the SUV in front of the house and turned off the ignition. "There are plenty of people who live in places like this. Besides, your aunt wouldn't bring Becca somewhere that wasn't safe."

"How do you know that? If she's joined a cult, she won't hesitate to bring a child into it." Jules unbuckled her seat belt and opened her door. "I'm going to find my daughter."

Mark fumbled with his seat belt then scrambled out of the SUV to catch up with Jules. He caught her by the elbow and pulled her to a stop.

"Take a deep breath and relax. Don't go storming in there like a madwoman. Let's get our bearings first."

"You get your bearings, Doctor, while I get my daughter."

Jules pulled away just as the front door opened.

"Jules! Welcome! I didn't know you were bringing someone with you," Aunt Val exclaimed as she waited for Jules in the open doorway.

"You didn't say I couldn't," Jules replied testily. "Is it allowed? Where's Becca?"

Val's brow furrowed, unimpressed by Jules' behavior.

"She's inside making cookies. Becca's been such a pleasure to have here. She's a wonderful child." Val extended her hand to Mark. "Hello, I'm Val Williams, Jules' aunt."

"Dr. Mark Blackwell," he said as he accepted Val's outstretched hand. "It's a pleasure to meet you." Mark turned and looked behind him. "This is quite the place you have here."

"It's not mine," Val chuckled as her hand touched the growing blush on her cheek, "although I do think of it as home. My boss, Dane, has made me feel like it is." She let go of his hand and gestured inside. "Come in out of the cold. I have a fresh pot of coffee brewing and Becca's made cookies. I'm glad you didn't try to drive out here last night. We had quite the blizzard. It took the men all morning to clear the snow."

Val took Jules' and Mark's coats, hanging them in the closet off the spacious stone foyer. "You can leave your boots by the door. The floors are heated so you'll be fine in your socks."

"Heated floors? That's a bit much, isn't it?" Jules asked as she slipped off her boots.

"It gets cold out here, Jules, and Dane needs the floors to be warm." Val gazed at her niece with concern. "What's wrong? You look upset. Paler than I remember."

"It's nothing," Jules lied, shaking her head.

"The gate is impressive," Mark offered. "And the driveway is longer than we expected."

"I'm sorry. I should have warned you about the drive. I sometimes forget the effect it can have on people. I remember the first time I drove here. I wondered if I had made a terrible mistake. The things that ran through my mind, I tell you. Silly me. Let's head to the kitchen."

"I've never heard you call your boss by his name until now."

"I haven't?" Val raised her fingertips to her mouth then smiled. "It must be because everyone calls him Boss."

Jules caught her reflection in the foyer's mirror. She adjusted the cowl of her navy blue sweater, satisfied that she didn't look too travel-weary despite being up most of the night at the hospital. Jules ran her fingers through her thick mane of red hair and reached into her jeans pants pocket, pulling out lip gloss. She applied it to her full lips.

"You look fine, dear. Besides, when have you worried about how you look? She's beautiful, isn't she Mark?"

"That she is," Mark said, giving Jules' a wide smile.

Val hooked her arm through Jules' arm and led her toward the kitchen. "This house was originally a log house built by Boss's great-great-grandparents. Every generation that followed added another extension to it. By the time Dane inherited the ranch, the house was a disaster. He's made remarkable changes to the place. Wait until you see the kitchen. He built it for me. He couldn't care less about all the appliances and gadgets as long as there's beer in the fridge and a snack cupboard filled for him and Lucky."

"Lucky?"

"His dog. Don't talk to Lucky or try to pet him, okay? Those are the only rules."

"Is he vicious?"

"Heaven's no, sweetheart. Lucky is a service dog. He's Dane's lifesaver."

Jules heard the sweet cadence of Becca's voice and a male's soft, easy laugh. She knew that laugh, or at least, it was similar to one she'd heard a long time ago. Jules felt butterflies in the pit of her stomach. After all this time, he still had a hold on her. She stopped short of the kitchen entrance.

"Are you okay?" Mark's hand gripped her shoulder.

She shook her head, hoping to clear her thoughts. It wasn't his voice she heard, only her imagination playing with her. "Yes, I'm fine.

Whatever it is, I'm sure Aunt Val's coffee and one of Becca's cookies will make me feel better."

"Mommy's here," Val announced when they arrived at the kitchen doorway.

Becca looked up, cookie dough smudged on her nose and showing a wide toothy smile. She kneeled on a stool at the kitchen island with an assortment of mixing bowls and cookie trays spread on the countertop.

"Mommy!"

"Hey, honey."

"Becca's in charge of spooning the dough onto the trays. She's quite precise in her measuring and shaping the cookies. She makes a pretty good dog bone," Val said, as she admired her grandniece's handiwork.

"I'm not surprised," Jules replied as her gaze searched for the owner of the male voice. His back was turned to her, hunched over the oven door as he removed a cookie sheet filled with cookies in the shape of dog bones. Her gaze stayed fixed on him, waiting to see him straighten, wishing to see those shoulders she first saw five years ago, and yet knowing that she would be disappointed. There would never be another man like Gary.

He straightened, revealing broad shoulders covered by a white T-shirt that stretched across his back, and jeans that clung to a very tight backside.

"Okay, this batch is ready," Dane announced as he turned to the counter. There was no mistaking her. She had haunted his dreams for the past five years. "Red."

"Gary."

"His name's Dane, Mommy. Not Gary. And Mommy's name is Mommy, not Red."

"You're right, honey," Jules said as she felt her knees give out from under her.

Mark, standing behind her, put his hands on her hips to support her. "Are you okay, Mommy?"

"Your Mommy has had a long drive. Aunt Val promised her coffee and one of your cookies," Mark said while guiding Jules to the kitchen counter. "Hi, I'm Dr. Mark Blackwell, a friend of Jules."

Dane placed the cookie tray on the counter and removed his oven mitts. "Dane Andrews," he said, his tone clipped. Fighting his need to keep his eyes on Jules, he offered his hand to Mark.

"Dane Andrews," Mark mused, as he shook Dane's hand while his other still held onto Jules. "I know that name."

"Little ears," Dane cautioned him, nodding toward Becca before he let go of Mark's hand.

"I have little ears," Becca piped in. "Lucky has big ears."

Val looked at Jules with concern. "Yes, he does," she agreed. "Why don't you two sit at the table and I'll get you coffee and some of Becca's cookies?"

Mark reached for one of the cookies on the counter. "Mind if I take one now?"

"They're doggie bones," Becca told him.

"I know, and they look delicious." Mark took a bite of the cookie and chewed. He grimaced as he tasted the cookie.

"Mark?" Jules asked, giving him a questioning look.

"Jules, they taste—"

"Like dog cookies," Dane said with amusement. "They're for my dog. If you'd listened to Becca, you would have saved yourself the embarrassment, Blackwell." Dane took a cookie from the counter and tossed it to his dog.

Val handed him a paper napkin. "Here, spit it into this."

"Too late. It's down. Coffee would help."

Becca laughed, her child's voice filling the kitchen and instantly easing the tension that had filled the room.

"Everyone, please take a seat at the table," Val said as her gaze moved from Jules to Dane, watching how they eyed each other.

Mark offered a chair to Jules at the large pine harvest table. He sat beside her, his gaze taking in the designer kitchen.

"This is quite the home you have here. Do you mind if I ask how big?"

"With all the additions, six thousand square feet."

"And the size of your spread?"

"Fifty-seven hundred hectares." Dane noticed Mark trying to figure out the size. "Fourteen hundred acres. For beef cattle. And other things," he said while removing the last dog bone from the cookie tray and placing it in a ceramic dog treat container. He turned his attention to Becca. "We're done. You know what that means?"

"Time for cookies and milk?"

"Exactly."

"I'll get everything. Dane, go sit at the table and visit." Val busied herself with gathering refreshments and putting cookies on a plate.

"I'll help." Dane's muscular frame came between Val and the cookies. Snatching the plate from the counter, he popped a cookie in his mouth before delivering it to the table.

Becca smiled at him with wide eyes. Dane took a seat opposite Jules.

"Can I sit on your knee?" Becca climbed on to his knee before Dane could answer.

"Becca?"

"It's okay," Dane said. "Unless, of course, you don't want her to."

"It's just that—"

"Mommy, can I have a doggie?"

"Not right now, Becca. We haven't moved into our house yet. And you're too little to look after one."

"I can look after Lucky."

"Lucky?"

Becca looked down at Dane's feet and pointed. "He's right there."

Jules peered under the table. "He's a big dog. Isn't he a bit heavy to be lying on your feet?"

"It's the best place for him to be," Dane answered.

"He's awfully quiet. What's that ridge of hair on his back?"

"Shh, Mommy," Becca whispered as she put her finger to her mouth. "He's working. Don't bother him."

Jules looked up at Dane who smiled at Becca.

"It's alright, Becca, your mommy can talk. He's a Rhodesian Ridgeback. His hair is like that naturally, and when he is agitated, or in protective mode, the hair stands up, making him look fierce. His breed originates from hunting lions."

"Is that so?" Mark asked, genuinely intrigued.

"He's not vicious?" Jules asked, showing concern for her daughter. "And he hunts lions?"

"She's safe with him. I guarantee it. Besides, we don't have lions out here. At least none that I know of." He winked at Jules and smiled.

Jules hadn't forgotten that wink. He had winked at her that night letting her know that she could relax in his company. She was safe with him. After all this time, Jules' body still reacted to it. She felt herself relax in her chair, the tension ease, although not leaving her entirely.

"Here you go," Val announced, placing a tray of mugs filled with steaming coffee on the table. "Help yourselves." She took her place at the table.

Dane picked up the plate of cookies and offered it to Jules. "I hear this is your favorite cookie. It's mine, too."

"Mine, too," Becca chirped.

"It seems you know more about me than I know about you," Jules murmured as she helped herself to an oatmeal raisin cookie.

"Only where cookies are concerned." Dane passed the plate to Mark.

"It looks like Becca's taken quite the shine to you," Mark said as he helped himself to a cookie before placing the plate on the table.

"They've been inseparable since she got here," Val answered. "And Dane's been wonderful with her. I don't know how many times he's listened to Red Riding Hood."

"You could have said no to her," Jules said.

"I could have, but I didn't want to. I've never won an argument with a redhead, no matter her size."

He took a bite from his cookie, taking a small piece on the outside and then worked his way around the cookie in a circular direction. Val noticed. So did Jules. Becca ate her cookie the same way while she sat on Dane's lap.

"I see she's shown you how to eat a cookie," Jules said, chuckling nervously.

Dane looked at her with bemusement. "This is the only way to eat a cookie."

"You and Becca are the only ones who do," Val replied.

"Must be a recessive gene," Mark offered. "Perhaps you and Becca share a gene from ancestors long ago."

Dane's gaze still focused on Jules. "That must be it."

He felt Lucky's paw on his lap and the nudge of his nose against his thigh. Dane looked down at his dog and shook his head.

"Now?" he asked the dog. "I have to go," he announced as he got to his feet. He placed Becca on his chair. "Tell Mommy what you did this morning while I'm gone, okay?"

"Can I come with you?"

"Not this time," Dane murmured as he patted the child's head. "If you'll excuse me. Val? Look after our guests, will you?"

Dane turned and left the kitchen with his dog at his side.

"What's wrong?" Jules asked her.

"He has to lie down," Becca answered sweetly. "Lucky makes him go to sleep."

Val smiled at Becca. Her innocence warmed her heart. "Dane has seizures. Lucky is trained to let him know when he's about to have one."

"Are they serious?"

"They must be if he has a service dog," Mark answered.

"He blacks out. Some days he'll only have one, and then there will be days where he has more." Val got to her feet to fetch the coffee pot. "He was in an accident, broadsided by a transport truck. He's lucky to have survived." She returned with the coffee and refilled their cups before placing the empty carafe on the table. "His life has improved greatly since he got Lucky."

"Aunt Val!"

"That sounds odd, doesn't it? I meant since he got the dog. Although Dane would agree that it was luck that got him that dog."

"When did he have the accident?"

"About five years ago. Dane has tried every medicine the doctors have prescribed. He's even tried cannabis, but it doesn't help. He blacks out. Just falls to the ground without any warning. Bates, he's Dane's assistant, found him in his bathroom one morning. He'd fallen and hit his head. The doctor told Dane he was lucky he didn't die. That's when Dane decided to get the service dog. He's been a blessing. Now Dane can finally have a life."

Jules did the math. Dane's accident happened after they had spent their night together.

Mark knew that Val needed to speak with Jules without Becca being present. The glances between the two women and the stilted conversation made it quite clear to the psychiatrist that there were issues that needed addressing. When Becca asked if she could color, he took the opportunity to go into the living room with her and supervise under the excuse that he heard it was the latest pastime for adults, too.

Val put the last of the dirty cups in the dishwasher then turned to face Jules who stared out the large window overlooking the snow-covered fields. Val leaned back against the counter, wringing the dishtowel in her hands for lack of knowing what else to do with them.

"She's his," Jules said softly, yet loud enough for Val to hear. "I never thought I'd see him again. I knew him as Gary. He helped me out of a bad situation and stayed with me for the night. I never thought I'd get pregnant. The doctors told me I couldn't. Remember?"

"Yes, I remember. You wouldn't tell us how it happened. Ned and I always wondered. I thought it was that doctor Sinclair, especially after Ned told me about him when you left. You let me believe that he was her father."

"You came up with your conclusions, Aunt Val."

"What else could I do when you wouldn't talk to me?"

Jules turned to face her aunt. Tears filled her eyes without falling. "I believed it was better to say nothing than to tell you the truth and have you believe I'd made the same mistake again. I couldn't tell you she was the product of a one night stand. Becca's a gift I thought I would never have. I didn't know her father, and I thought I'd never see him again. I was happy with that."

"You could have told us. There would have been no judgment." Val folded the towel and placed it on the counter by the sink. She sighed heavily. "What's done is done. No more dwelling on the past. At least my hunch was confirmed."

"You knew Becca is Dane's?"

"Not until now. Although," Val smiled as something came to mind, "the way she ate her cookie when we were having tea in your hotel suite. There was something about it that reminded me of someone. It wasn't until I saw her with Dane that I wondered about the possibility. They have some of the same mannerisms, Jules. It's uncanny."

Jules' gaze went to the hallway. "Do you think Dane knows?"

"Dane?" Val gave a knowing smile. "Of course he does. Why do you think he spent so much time with Becca? The man's smart. It was part of his job to observe people. Learn everything about them. He could see himself in her without even trying. They eat their cookies the same way, for heaven's sake! I mean what other person eats a cookie in such a strange way. They are both left-handed. Here's the kicker, Jules. They have the same shaped ears. Look at them and tell me they aren't the same."

"What did he say?"

"He didn't say a word. He's cool that way. I'm sure he knew as soon as you arrived here any questions he had would get answered."

"I have questions now." Dane's voice was low and demanding.

Both women turned their attention to the doorway to find Dane standing with Lucky by his side. Dane's hair was damp. He had showered and changed his clothes.

"Val? If you don't mind Jules and I will be in my office. Look after my daughter and Dr. Blackwell. Please. Red?" He held his hand out to Jules.

Jules felt the heat rush to her cheeks. With her head held high and shoulders back, she walked to him. After all this time, her body still obeyed him. She took his hand and looked at his face, holding his brown-eyed gaze with her emerald eyes.

"How are you feeling?" she asked softly.

"Are you asking me as Red or as Jules?"

"Both. I was never anyone but myself with you."

"I feel like a truck hit me. Not quite a semi, but enough of one to make my head spin."

"Do you always feel like that after a seizure?"

"Never. It's from having two redheads walk into my crosshairs." Dane pointed down the hallway towards his office.

Lucky followed them, the sound of his toenails clicking on the hardwood floor.

Jules looked over her shoulder at the massive dog following them.

"Don't mind him, Red, he keeps all my secrets." They reached his office. "After you." Dane opened the door and stood back to let Jules enter.

Dane watched Jules take a few steps into the room and stop. He heard the soft gasp escape from her when she took notice of the photographs and memorabilia arranged meticulously on his bookshelves and the mantle above the fireplace. There was no hiding from her now, no pretending that he was the bush firefighter who satisfied her fantasies.

He closed the heavy wooden door behind him and leaned against it and waited. Dane knew there was no easy way to tell Jules who he was. What he was. It was best to have Jules see for herself before they talked. She could make the first move as she did when they first met.

Jules stepped toward the bookcase displaying various leather-bound books and framed photographs. She reached for the one that caught her attention first. It was a photograph of five people dressed in military desert khaki somewhere in the Middle East. Four of the people were men, carrying rifles of some kind. The fifth was a woman. She stood at the end of the row beside Dane. They were all smiles.

Jules felt the bile rise from her stomach. She placed the photograph back on the shelf.

"You killed people."

"I prevented good people from being killed."

"By killing other people," Jules said accusingly.

"Yes."

"How many did you kill?"

"I don't know."

Jules spun around to face Dane. Her eyes wild with emotion. "I'm not stupid. Mark recognized your name. You're a famous sniper! You must have counted every single one of your kills. That's what people like you do, isn't that right?"

Dane shook his head. "It's not important."

"It's important to me! Don't you think I should know how many people the father of my child has killed?"

She held his gaze. Dane refused to look away. He never felt ashamed about his kill record, and he would be damned if he would let her make him feel that way now.

"Four hundred fifty-two."

Jules stepped back, her legs weakening beneath her. Dane moved to save her from falling and was stopped by her outstretched hand.

"Don't touch me."

"Sit down then. Let's talk about it." He gestured toward the leather sofa. "How about a drink? I know I could use one."

"Okay." Jules made her way to the sofa. She noticed the quality of the leather, and the luxurious comfort the large piece of furniture offered. It reminded her of another sofa. "Your condo," she said as she watched him pour drinks from a crystal decanter, "it had the same sofa."

"I like my comforts." He turned to face her. Jules' eyes no longer burned with anger. Now they watched him with suspicion, letting him know that this was his moment to talk, to make her see him as more than the killer she perceived.

He offered Jules her drink. "May I sit with you?"

She nodded yes.

Dane took his seat and Lucky lay down and rested his head on Dane's feet. Dane made sure to keep a few inches from Jules, fully aware that a neutral zone would be necessary. She was beautiful. More beautiful than he remembered. Motherhood agreed with her. He wondered if he voiced his thoughts she'd take them as a compliment. Everything about her was perfect. Dane prided himself on his attention to details. He had memorized everything about his Red only to discover that she had changed for the better. Her eyes still sparkled, but there was something about them now. They reminded him of a wildcat—that of a mother cat when protecting her young, her eyes wild with a threatening ferocity.

"Val told me about how you lost your parents. I can understand why you hate guns."

"Hate?" Jules scoffed. "I loathe guns, and I hate people who think they have the right to own them. Nothing good comes from owning a gun. Only death and destruction of innocent lives."

Dane took in a deep breath. She wasn't going to make this easy. He would have been surprised if she had. "Your parents were gunned down by a madman. Someone who didn't care who he killed as long as he killed. There is no excuse for what he did, and I am sorry that you had to suffer because of him."

"He shot my parents and twenty others in cold blood because he was unhappy with his employer. If he didn't have a gun—" Jules looked away from him and stared at the window without seeing beyond the glass.

"I agree."

"What?" His words pulled her attention back to him.

"I said, I agree. Most people don't need to own guns. They are unnecessary. Their only purpose should be for warfare."

"I don't like wars either."

"And yet, we have them."

Jules drank from her glass, finishing it in one swallow. She placed the empty glass on the table beside her before making herself comfortable on the sofa. Dane mirrored her, finishing his drink then placing the glass on the table at his side.

"What made you decide to kill people?" She kept her gaze focused on him, trying to read the man who she now saw as a stranger.

Dane groaned and shook his head. "My enlisting was never about killing people. I joined the Navy as part of my university education. Through my training, I discovered that I had a knack for shooting, and I ended up in sniper detail. That's how I met Bates. We were a team."

"You knew you would kill people."

"Yes. And I knew that I would be saving lives, too. My unit, everyone in our camp, and the local villagers—I kept them safe. I won't apologize for what I've done."

"Were you ever shot?"

"Shot at, but never hit. I was one of the lucky ones."

Jules pulled her legs up underneath her. She hugged her legs and rested her chin on her knees. Her gaze softened.

Dane remembered this—how Jules could look at him and make him feel as though she was looking into him and seeing what was wrong with him.

"Your seizures—Aunt Val told me that a transport truck hit you."

"My truck was totaled, and I ended up in a coma for a few weeks and afterward, rehab. My body is pretty much back to normal except for this." Dane pointed to his temple.

"Drugs don't help?"

"Not much. That's why I have this guy." Dane reached down and scratched the top of Lucky's head. "He's my alarm system. I've got five minutes to find cover. I wish it were more time, but I can't complain. Five minutes is better than falling flat on my face."

"Your accident was after we met."

"Nothing gets by you, does it, Red?" Dane teased as he leaned back into the comfort of the sofa. "Yes, it was the day after I met you. I've been trying to get my life back on track ever since." He held her gaze, hoping she would see how much their meeting had affected him.

"You look as though you have it back. This place—"

"I had this place before my accident. It's the things I've had to give up and what I'm trying to get back."

"Such as?"

"There's my work."

"Which is?"

Dane knew the conversation was coming to this and there was no way to avoid it. He got to his feet, picked up his glass. "Care for a refill?" He held out his free hand to her for the empty glass.

She handed her glass to him. "Make it a double this time. Please."

Dane poured their drinks then returned to the sofa. He gave Jules her glass, and remained standing, looking down at her. "Still holding to the belief that you don't get drunk?"

She rolled her eyes. "Do you remember everything about our night together?"

"You're a hard woman to forget, Red, even with a brain injury."

She took a long sip of her drink. "You know, you're the only man who has ever called me Red."

"Good." Dane took his seat beside her, sitting closer. "The bar where we met. I own it."

Jules nodded. "That explains the service we were getting."

"My staff treats every customer the same."

"Not that well."

"Maybe. They know I expect the best from them."

"So that's it? You own a bar?"

"The bar's a sideline. I've always liked the place, and I bought it when the owner decided to retire."

"You're a homeboy? I wonder why we never bumped into each other?" She sighed. "I guess that's because I spent most of my time at the hospital saving lives and you were—"

"Doing my part to save lives."

She sighed, then took another sip from her glass. "I'll never accept what you did."

Dane rubbed at his forehead, wondering if he should continue this conversation or find a safer, neutral territory.

"What's wrong?"

"Full steam ahead," he uttered.

Dane swallowed the last of his drink and set the glass down on the table. He shifted in his seat to face Jules. What needed to be said had to be done face to face. He had to see her reaction, knowing her facial expression would tell him more than any words she threw at him.

"I didn't plan to be in the bar the night we met. A client canceled a meeting last minute, and so Bates and I ended up at the bar for drinks."

"So I guess I should thank that client of yours. If it weren't for him, I wouldn't have Becca."

"That's one way of looking at it."

"Your client. Why were you meeting?"

He took the glass from her hand and placed it on the table. Taking her hands in his he gripped them, hoping to keep her attention on him.

"We were supposed to finalize my next assignment. My other job is government-sanctioned. It's highly classified. It's almost like firefighting, the job you gave to Gary. I put out dangerous fires except that—"

Jules closed her eyes. "Don't say it. Please don't say it."

"I killed people, Red. I killed evil people."

"No," she cried. "Don't."

"I haven't worked since my accident. Now I train others to do my job. It's my business."

"That's what you miss doing? Killing?"

"It's not that simple."

Jules opened her eyes wide. "You're a monster."

Dane's grip tightened on her. "I don't take life lightly. I killed the monsters who preyed on their people—the despots, the dictators who bled their people dry and then demanded more. I killed the monsters who kidnapped children as innocent as Becca and turned them into sex slaves. I'd still be doing it if it weren't for this damned head injury. I can't risk my life or the life of my men if I can't stay conscious."

Jules looked down at her hands, held firmly in his. She remembered a time when she ached to feel his touch, to be in his arms and feel safe. Now, she questioned everything she had thought about him.

"Aunt Val? She knows?"

"Yes."

"From the very beginning?"

"Yes."

"Why didn't she tell me?"

"She couldn't. She knew the secrets she'd have to keep. Val came here with her eyes wide open, Jules."

"My aunt would never support killing. Her sister, my mother, was gunned down in cold blood. How could she ever say that killing was okay?"

"That's a conversation you'll have to have with her."

"No, this isn't right."

Jules pulled her hands out of Dane's grip and looked away from him, focusing her attention once again on the large floor to ceiling windows. She scrambled off the sofa and headed to one of the windows. She peered outside. Snow. Mountains. Wide open space. Plenty of spots for a shooter to hide and wait. Jules moved away from the window.

"Could we ever be in danger? Is that why you've got such high security around this place?"

Dane shrugged and exhaled roughly. "My identity is kept secret. No one is in danger here."

"So why all the hi-tech security?"

"Just in case I'm wrong."

"What if you're wrong now and Becca's life is in danger? My god, why did I let her come here!"

Dane got to his feet quickly, almost tripping over his dog. He reached out for her, grabbing her shoulders with his strong hands.

"I would never let anything happen to you, Val, or Becca. All of you are safer here than crossing the street. You can trust me on that."

"I don't think so, asshole."

"Red, you of all people know that there are no guarantees in life. You can't always guarantee that you can prevent people from dying. No matter how hard we try to do the right thing, bad things happen. You know that as well as I do. Your parents went on a holiday and died because they were in the wrong place at the wrong time. No one could have seen that coming. I managed to serve four tours without getting shot, but I got my bell rung at home, and my life almost turned to shit. There are no sure things. We can only do the best that we can."

"Everything about you goes against everything that I believe in." Jules dropped her gaze to the floor. "I can't even look at you right now."

"We have to talk about Becca."

"No. Not today. I'm taking Becca away from here." She tried to step away from him, but his grip kept her in place. "Please let me go."

"Promise me that we'll talk. About Becca. Please." Dane's hands dropped to his side while he searched her face for a trace of understanding.

"I can't make any promises right now." Jules made her way to the door and opened it. "Please don't follow me. I'm taking Becca home, and I don't want her to see you."

"This is my house."

"And she is my daughter, and I don't want her anywhere near you. Not right now."

"She's my daughter, too. You can't keep me from her," Dane warned, his voice threatening.

"I can for today. Let us leave, Dane, before words get said that can't be taken back."

Chapter Five

THERE WAS A CHILLED SILENCE that filled the foyer, one that warned Val and Mark that one uttered word would bring another onslaught of cutting words from the angry redhead. Becca sobbed uncontrollably on the stone floor crying out for Dane and Lucky as her mother's experienced and gentle hands coaxed her body into her winter coat. Mark gave an embarrassed goodbye to Val before heading out with Becca's bag to the waiting SUV warming up to fight the winter cold of the late afternoon.

Aunt Val wiped away her tears with the back of her hand, tears caused by the angry accusation of, "How could you!" and the sudden announcement of their departure. Memories of Jules' temper reminded Val that it was useless to argue with her. She would have to give her niece time to cool down before attempting to contact her.

Dane watched the SUV head away from the house down the long driveway. He watched from his office, alone and angry. Although Becca had only been under his roof for twenty-four hours, the house now felt cold and empty without her. He was mad that Jules forbade him from saying goodbye to Becca. He was angrier with himself for not standing up to her.

Dane felt the wet nose of his four-legged companion against the back of his hand. He looked down to find Becca's bunny in Lucky's mouth. Flopsy. Becca didn't go anywhere without that beloved stuffed animal.

Dane took the offered toy from Lucky's mouth and smiled. "I think we'll be seeing her sooner than later, boy."

A light knock at his door turned Dane's attention away from the window.

"Val."

"What happened?"

Dane gestured to an armchair facing his desk. "Care to join me for a drink?" He set the toy down on his desk.

Val nodded and made her way to her chair. She fell into it slowly and released a frustrated sigh. "Did you fight over Becca?"

Dane finished pouring their drinks. Handing Val her glass, he answered, "We didn't even get there. I'm a murderer in Jules' eyes. There was no convincing her otherwise."

"You're a hero! Doesn't she realize how many lives you've saved?"

"It's the number I've taken that's the problem." Dane took a sip from his glass before sitting down in his leather chair. "It doesn't sit well with someone who has dedicated her life to saving lives."

Val shook her head. "She's a smart woman. She should know that it's necessary—"

"Nope. Killing is killing. I'm as bad as the man who killed her parents. I'm probably worse because I got paid for it."

"She must hate me for not telling her."

"You couldn't tell her."

"Yes, but—"

"You're family. She came back to High River because of you. She'll get over it."

"We've only just reconciled. I wouldn't be too sure about that."

"Well, she'll have to see one of us before too long. I've got something she wants."

"What's that?"

Dane picked up the stuffed bunny he'd placed on his desk. "This."

Once Becca had cried herself to sleep, Mark waited for what he thought was an acceptable amount of time before he dared to speak to Jules.

"Do you want to talk about it?"

"There's nothing to say," Jules answered flatly, staring out her passenger window.

"It must have been quite a shock—"

"I said I don't want to talk about it. Please, Mark, I've got things to think through."

"I could help as a friend. I'll put my psychiatrist's hat away. I promise."

She turned to him and smiled. Jules reached for his hand and held it. "Thank you. I know you want to help me, and I appreciate it. This is something I have to work out for myself."

"You don't have to do everything alone, you know. Have some trust in the people around you that they can help you."

Jules shook her head. "I know that. It's not that easy. Not this time." She turned her head and looked out at the snowy winter landscape and wondered what the hell her aunt was thinking. Today's Aunt Val wasn't the Aunt Val she remembered. The Aunt Val she knew was anti-violence, fundraised for her church, and wrote letters to politicians asking for their support of stricter gun legislation. Did something happen to her when Uncle Ned died? Did she have a mini-stroke?

Jules should have taken the first flight back to Alberta when her aunt told her she was moving in with a stranger to be his housekeeper.

Jules felt the heaviness of regret seep into her bones. She would have insisted on meeting Val's employer, and then she would have met Gary. His real name was Dane. Time had not changed him. He looked as perfect as she remembered, if not more so. His T-shirt showed off every muscle hidden beneath the stretched material. His hair was still cropped short, although he now sported a light beard. Damn him for looking that good. As much as Jules wanted to hate the man for the killer he was, she knew that if he hadn't come to her rescue that night, her world would be a much different one. A world without Becca.

"Do you mind dropping us off at the entrance?"

"Let me help you with Becca. She's quite the armful."

"I know, but I can manage. It's been a long day, and all I want to do is get her settled in bed before I take a long hot bath."

Mark did as he was asked by stopping at the hotel's entrance long enough to help Jules gather Becca and her bag in her arms. He kissed her on the forehead before saying goodnight.

"Call me?"

"Tomorrow once I've had a chance to sort things out. I promise."

It wasn't until Jules had returned to her hotel suite and unpacked Becca's little travel bag that she realized Flopsy was missing. She called Mark in a panic.

"Where is he?" Becca cried with tears running down her cheeks.

"I don't know, sweetheart," Jules answered. She hugged her daughter while she waited for Mark to check his car for the missing toy. She heard him curse while he searched.

"I don't see him," frustration added an edge to his voice.

"Are you sure?"

"I've torn my car apart, Jules. The damned rabbit is not here. If you don't have it, then there's only one place it could be."

Jules groaned. She didn't want to accept that her daughter's long-eared companion had been left behind in enemy territory. There was no way in hell she'd return to the ranch for a stuffed animal.

"Mommy!"

"I have to go. Thanks for looking."

"Call your aunt, Jules. Don't punish Becca because you're pissed at Val. Call her. I'll talk to you tomorrow."

"Okay. Good night, Mark."

Becca's bottom lip quivered. "Did he find Flopsy?"

"I think Flopsy is with Auntie Val, sweetheart. We must have left him behind."

"No," the child wailed. "I have to have him." She sobbed, clinging to her mother. "He's all alone!"

Jules hugged her daughter tighter and kissed the top of her head. A lost bunny was a terrible end to a terrible day. She didn't know how much more of this upset she could take.

Her cellphone buzzed, indicating an incoming text. Jules looked at her phone and saw the image of the missing Flopsy beside the caller's number.

She clicked open the message, " *I want to come home. Lucky thinks I'm a new chew toy. The asshole is threatening to tie me to a post and shoot me. He wants another chance to talk to you or else. I miss Becca. How is she?*"

"Asshole's right," she muttered as she typed in her reply, "*Becca is devastated. Please don't hurt Flopsy. If you can manage to drag yourself away from your fortress and promise not to kill anyone on your way here, please release him into my care.*"

"*Done.*"

There was a knock at the door.

"What now?" Jules groaned in frustration.

"Mommy?"

"Hush, sweetie. Someone's at the door." She pulled the door open wide as she grumbled, "Who is it?"

Damn him. He had to be a smart ass by sending the text from outside her hotel suite. Double damn him for looking so damned sexy as though he stepped out of a men's fashion magazine and landed at her door wearing a sheepskin coat, unbuttoned, that showed a white buttoned shirt underneath. His jeans were like the ones she remembered him wearing—showing off all of his attributes. One hand held his Stetson, and the other held the leash attached to Lucky.

"He's wearing a jacket," Jules remarked, noticing Lucky's red coat.

"It's his service vest. He needs it when we go out. Otherwise, people won't know why there's an a-hole lying unconscious on the ground with this ferocious beast on top of him."

"He's not ferocious."

"Glad you think so."

Becca turned to face the voice at the door. "Dane! Did you find Flopsy?"

"Lucky did, sweetheart. That's why we're here." He pulled the bunny from the inside pocket of his coat and handed it to her.

"Flopsy!" Becca cried out as she hugged the stuffed toy.

"Are you going to invite us in, or is this how we make the exchange?"

Jules stepped back, allowing Dane and Lucky entrance to her suite. She let Becca down who immediately hugged Lucky.

"Thank you, Lucky. You saved Flopsy."

"He sure did," Dane said appreciatively. He bent down and removed Lucky's leash. "I don't know where he found the little guy, but I'm sure glad he did. Did you miss your bunny?"

Becca nodded her head, still hugging the dog's neck with the bunny sandwiched between them. "He's my best friend."

"Thank you. Becca's been upset since she realized Flopsy was missing."

"I think there's been a lot of upset today."

"Yes, there has." Jules closed the door. "Would you like a drink? I think we both could use one."

"I hope we don't always have to have alcohol when we're together," he teased. "It's not always the best foundation for a relationship. And yet, I think we can thank a bottle of Remy Martin for making us parents of this little one." Dane shrugged off his coat and placed it and his Stetson on a chair by the door.

"We weren't drunk."

"I didn't say we were."

"I don't have any hard liquor. Will red wine do? I have a nice bottle of Merlot."

"Sure. Thanks."

Dane looked around the hotel suite. It was acceptable for one of the city's mainstream hotels, although not on the same level as his condo.

"How long will you and Becca be staying here?"

"Hopefully, one more week. I'm having some minor repairs done to my townhouse before we move in."

"You're welcome to stay in my condo if you'd like."

"Thank you, but no. We'll be fine here."

Dane turned his attention to Becca. She'd curled up beside Lucky with one arm draped around Lucky's neck and the other clinging to her bunny. "Let's put her to bed so that we can talk." Dane made his way to them and crouched beside Lucky and the sleepy child. "Stay," he said softly to Lucky as he scooped Becca up in his arms. "Where to?" he asked Jules.

"She's in here," Jules said as she led him to the bedroom.

Jules pulled back the duvet then stood back to let Dane place Becca on the bed. She covered Becca with the duvet then kissed her on her forehead. "Sweet dreams, baby."

Dane waited for Jules to step back before he leaned over and kissed Becca on her cheek. "'Night, Becca. Daddy loves you."

He followed Jules out to the living area and took a seat on the small couch that was part of a small seating area.

"Come here, boy."

Lucky came to Dane and sat by his feet.

"He's very well trained."

"He has to be. My life depends on it. He'll warn me before I turn into the big unconscious asshole on the floor."

"That's not funny."

"Well, you didn't disagree with me when I first said it, although I'm glad you don't think my dog is ferocious."

Jules handed him his glass of wine. Noticing that there wasn't much room left for her to sit beside Dane without sitting on his lap, she opted for one of the armchairs facing him.

"Thank you for returning Flopsy. I hope it wasn't too much of an inconvenience for you."

"Family is never an inconvenience." He took a sip of his wine, nodding his head in appreciation. "Very nice."

"Thanks. It's one of my favorites."

"I'll have to remember that. Speaking of favorites and family," Dane paused while he stretched out his long legs in front of him, "Your favorite aunt could do with a phone call, maybe one with an apology. I'll leave that up to you."

"I'll think about it."

"She said you'd say that. It seems Val knows you pretty well for not having had much contact with you in the last couple of years."

Jules watched him with wary eyes. The man she had asked to rescue her from a bad situation and who eagerly obliged her, the man who played along with being her fantasy boyfriend for one perfect night seemed to be playing with her now. He seemed too relaxed, too comfortable in her presence, especially after what she had said to him earlier. This time Jules could only see him as a stranger, a man she didn't know, and one she should handle with caution.

"Did Val tell you why we had a falling out?"

"Not really. Something about a difference of opinion."

Jules chuckled.

"Care to let me in on the joke?"

Jules finished the contents of her glass before answering him. "After Uncle Ned died, I asked Val to move out to Toronto to live with us. I thought it would be good for her. Instead, she told me she didn't want to leave High River because it was her home."

"I'm sure it was a difficult decision for her. She thinks of you as her daughter."

"I know that, and I accepted her decision. It's what she said to me after that caused us to become estranged."

"And that was?"

"You honestly have no idea?"

"Tell me."

"She chose you over Becca and me to become your housekeeper."

"I didn't know." Dane saw the doubt cross her face. "I swear to you. I had no idea you were her niece. We ran a thorough background check on her. The Jules Montgomery in her file is not you."

"I find that hard to believe."

"Do you think that I hired Val knowing she was related to you? Why would I do that? And why in hell would I not contact you?"

"Maybe you forgot about me. Your brain injury—"

"I may have forgotten a lot of things when I got hit, but believe me, you were never one of them." He closed his eyes, forcing himself to recall seeing Val's file. "Bates checked you out himself. He told me you wouldn't be a problem."

"Bates?"

"My right-hand man. Do you remember the man who was sitting beside me in the bar the night we met?"

"No."

Dane shook his head. "It doesn't matter. He was there that night. He kept an eye on us, making sure that creep didn't cause us any trouble."

"So?"

"Bates knew what you looked like, so if he came across your picture with Val's, he would have made the connection."

"Why wouldn't he have told you?"

"That's a good question. It's something we'll discuss on our drive home." Dane got to his feet and retrieved the opened bottle of wine. He filled Jules' glass and then his own, finishing the bottle.

Dane reached out to Jules and touched her hair. The red waves felt exactly how he remembered them—silky soft and thick.

Jules leaned into his hand. She couldn't help herself. Her body had missed his touch.

"I've never stopped thinking of you, Red. If I had known you were Val's niece, I would have contacted you right away."

"I didn't trick you into getting me pregnant."

"The thought never crossed my mind."

"When I was a teenager, I got pregnant. There were complications. I lost the baby and almost died after the delivery. My doctor told me that there was too much internal scarring and that I'd never get pregnant again."

"What do doctors know? Right?"

Jules gave him a sad smile.

"What are you thinking?" Dane released her hair then took his seat on the couch.

"You're the father of my child, and I don't know anything about you."

"Don't kid yourself. You know me. The man you asked to rescue you five years ago is the same man sitting in front of you now. I may have been pretending to be Gary, the bush firefighter, but there was nothing disingenuous about me. How I spoke to you, treated you—that was all me, no pretending. And I know you weren't faking it with me."

"And yet there's another side to you, one that I didn't see and one that I can't accept."

"It's not another side. It's all me."

Jules looked away from him, shaking her head.

"Jules, look at me." His voice was steady, demanding. "When a man senses that a woman can see right into his soul and she doesn't flinch, he never forgets her. You looked deep into my soul, and you saw me. All of me. That I know and I would stake my life on it."

"One night together doesn't make us soulmates."

"We were pretty damn close. Is that what you have with the psychiatrist?"

"Mark? No! We're friends, nothing more."

"Does he know that?"

"Yes, he most certainly does." Her eyes opened wide when she realized something. "You're jealous of him."

"I don't want him to be first in line to be Becca's father. That spot is mine."

"Fatherhood has to be earned. DNA isn't the only requirement."

Dane finished the contents of his glass. "We made a baby who happens to be the smartest most adorable little girl I have ever seen. I'm her father. There's no disputing that. I plan to be in her life, and yours, too, if you'll let me. I can handle you not wanting me as a lover, but I won't let you keep me out of Becca's life. I've already missed out on too much."

"She's not always adorable, you know. Having a very bright child can be challenging."

"Like reading Little Red Riding Hood countless times?"

"That's the latest favorite. You haven't heard Becca read Goldilocks and the Three Bears."

"I can't wait."

She could see it in his eyes—the sadness in knowing that he had missed out on Becca's first years. If she were honest with herself, she had to admit that she felt the same knowing that Becca's father was missing out on this unique child.

"I've thought about you often, especially when Becca does something that I don't recognize in myself. I wondered if it was a part of you."

"Why didn't you—"

"Try to find you and tell you that you got a one night stand pregnant?"

"You were never a one night stand."

"I didn't know what we were, Gary." She didn't correct herself. To her, he was Gary. Her Gary. "We happened by chance. We didn't know anything about each other. I didn't want to burden you with a baby."

"A child is not a burden."

"I never thought of her as one."

"You found me once. You could have done it again."

"No, I couldn't. You said so yourself that I was lucky to find you that night. And besides," Jules took a sip from her glass, "deep down, I didn't want to."

Dane let out a ragged breath as he leaned into the back of the couch, his gaze focused on her.

"You were a fantasy—one perfect night. I didn't want to ruin my memory of you by being disappointed by your reaction to my pregnancy. If you had rejected us, I wouldn't have been able to bear it."

"I would never have rejected you. You've always been with me."

"It's easy to say that now."

He shook his head. "No, I've always felt that way. After we spent our night together, I woke up missing you. It took a run-in with a truck and a knock to my head to make me realize that I needed to get my life on track so that I could be with a woman like you."

"Did you find her?"

Dane gazed down at his hands. It had been too long since he'd felt the softness of a woman's skin or the touch of a woman. "You're a hard woman to replace." He shrugged. "It looks like you've moved on."

Jules opened her mouth to speak and then changed her mind. "It's getting late."

"We haven't talked about Becca. It was part of our deal."

"Another time, okay?"

"I want to spend time with her. As her father. We have to tell her who I am."

"No. Not right now."

"Why? What's wrong with telling her? She likes me. She loves my dog. What's wrong with telling her now?"

"I want to talk to Mark first."

"Why? As your boyfriend or as a psychiatrist?"

"If you'd let me finish." Her glare silenced him. "Mark is a child psychiatrist, and I trust his advice. He may suggest that we wait until Becca gets settled in her new home and gets to know you before we spring it on her that you're her father. It may be too much for her to process."

"That's bullshit. Becca didn't have any trouble riding in a stranger's car or spending the night in a stranger's home. You put her in Val's care, and Becca trusted that she was safe. Which she was. Telling her that I'm her father will be received the same way. She trusts you, Jules. And she trusts me."

Jules got to her feet. "Sorry. I'm not ready to tell her."

"Not ready, or you don't want to?"

Her chin lifted in defiance. "I'm her mother. I get to decide if and when I tell her."

Dane stood up and stepped toward her. Jules held her ground, her back straightening.

"It's because of what I do. Isn't it? You don't want her to have a father who's a trained killer. You'd rather she had a shrink for one."

"I never said that."

"You didn't have to. I can see it in your eyes, the way you look at me."

"I've had a lot to deal with today. You can't expect me to make a decision right away because you want it. Becca is my responsibility. Mine alone. And I am not going to let just anyone into her life because of his DNA."

Jules was exhausted. Tears formed in her eyes, threatening to fall. She needed him gone. She needed to be alone, with time to think about the man who had haunted her dreams.

Dane reached for Jules. His hands grabbed her upper arms. As he leaned into her, his nose almost touched hers. "Let me remind you that when you approached me in my bar, you had no clue as to who I was or what I did. You didn't care as long as I'd pretend to be your boyfriend so that creep would give up and leave you alone. You never once asked me what I did. You didn't care as long as you got what you wanted. Someone to keep you company, make you feel safe, and make love to you so for once in a very long time you wouldn't feel alone when you went to sleep."

"I wouldn't have stayed with you if I'd known what you did."

"You knew, or at least the thought crossed your mind. Do you remember me offering to take care of the creep and you asked if I was going to kill him? You asked me more than once how I would deal with him. Admit it, Red, somewhere deep inside you knew what kind of man I was."

"I never."

"You didn't lie to me then, don't start now. We played a game, but don't kid yourself. We never cheated. Everything we said about ourselves was true. Every way we reacted to each other's touch, body, smile, was genuine. That night, I knew a helluva lot about you, and you knew more about me than any woman has. It didn't matter that we didn't know each other's name, we knew each other on the inside, and that is more than most couples ever do."

He kissed her. God help him. He couldn't help himself. The way she glared at him in defiance, pretending that there was nothing between them when he knew to his very core that there was. Her denial demanded punishment of the most sensual kind. His hard mouth covered hers, he tasted red wine and the salt of her tears.

Jules softened in his arms. His mouth was hard against hers. She fought against giving in to him, and yet her body betrayed her, remembering what it felt like to be held by him and to be kissed by him. Her lips parted, allowing his tongue to taste her. She heard his soft moan and answered with hers. His scent filled her—musk, man, and scotch mixed with red wine. An unusual taste, but one that suited him, and made her want more.

He released her—first his mouth and then his strong hands. Dane took a step back, his gaze fixed on hers.

Jules' green eyes sparkled, betraying her emotions. "What do you want from me?"

"I want my daughter. And I want you."

She shook her head. "I can't."

"You will."

Dane turned from her and headed toward the door. Lucky followed close behind him. Dane shrugged on his coat and put on his Stetson.

"Time to go home, boy," he said softly to his dog as he clipped on his leash. "By the way, whatever happened to that creep?"

Jules gasped, her head snapping to attention. "He ended up in the hospital that night. My uncle told me that he was mugged. You didn't—"

"I was with you the entire night. I couldn't have. Anything else?"

"He left High River General and started up a practice of his own."

"Interesting."

"Are you sure you had nothing to do with what happened to him?"

"I may have a brain injury, but I would know if and when I had someone beaten. I haven't laid eyes on the man since that night at the bar. He probably had some real boyfriends waiting to tell him to leave their girlfriends alone." Dane smiled at the thought. "Goodnight, Red. I'll be in touch."

Chapter Six

BATES WAITED FOR DANE, the man he always referred to as Boss, in the heated comfort of the black SUV. He had kept the engine running, thinking that Boss's visit with the fiery redhead would be short and to the point. Hand over the stuffed toy, tell the woman she was whacko, then say goodbye. Boss didn't need a woman like that in his life. He needed someone calmer, kinder, and accepting. He should have known the doctor was trouble the moment he saw her hug Boss from behind and pull him into a game that lasted for hours. She had a stalker, a co-worker who didn't take the hint that she wasn't interested. Bates couldn't blame the beautiful doctor for attracting danger, but he could blame her for asking Boss to come to her rescue. Boss didn't need to prove himself a hero. Those who knew him and worked with him witnessed his heroics daily.

Bates remembered that night as though he were a fly on the wall, watching without being noticed. He kept an eye on Boss and the red-headed beauty who had grabbed his attention. Bates liked her. He had to admit for a few hours it was good to see Boss happy. Boss danced with her, drank with her, and he laughed. It had been a long time since he'd seen Boss laugh.

Their line of work had taken its toll on them, especially Bates. Boss promised Bates that he'd always have his six and he kept his word by hiring him as his right-hand man. In return, Bates made it his mission to keep a watchful eye on Boss and to keep him out of harm's way, even if it meant running interference with a redheaded beauty.

Her stalker, Dr. John Sinclair, was relentless. Bates had to give him credit for not giving up. He smiled as he thought of him. Instead of leaving the bar with his tail between his legs, he kept coming back for more, thinking that he could get the better of Boss. Bates wouldn't allow that. Instead, when Bates caught the man lurking in the shadows outside the bar, he made his move to teach the jerk a lesson. The doctor had a glass jaw, falling unconscious to the ground with one right hook to the face. Bates gathered up his crumpled form and stashed him in the trunk of his car. Knowing that Boss would be spending the rest of the night with the woman, Bates was free to carry out his plan. He didn't take him far, only to the seediest part of Calgary where he dumped him in an alley without his wallet or his cellphone. What happened next was all up to the doctor.

The rear door to the SUV swung open. He heard Boss order the dog onto the back seat. The door slammed, and then the front passenger door opened, and a furious Boss dropped into the passenger seat.

"You have some explaining to do, my friend. Out with it now, or I swear I will beat the shit out of you when we get home."

Bates was the bigger and stronger of the two men, although Boss was the dirtier fighter. Bates knew he could hold his own against his friend, and yet there was no way in hell he would ever hit back.

"I knew the woman was Val's niece."

"Her name is Jules."

"After your accident, you were saying crazy shit while you were coming out of your coma. Sometimes you'd say the word red. And then you started talking about a woman. I put two and two together and figured it was the woman from the bar. She made you happy, Boss. I could see it that night."

"She did. Keep going."

"When I ran the background check, I recognized her right away. Val told us that she had one living relative, a niece, and they were estranged. I thought it would work."

"What would work?"

"You and the doctor could reconnect once you got better."

"Then why would you keep her from me?"

"You weren't ready. And now. . ."

"Now?"

"She didn't exactly fall into your arms, did she?"

Dane leaned back in his seat. He blew out in frustration. "No."

"She's not the one for you."

"That's not for you to say."

"She doesn't accept what you do. How can you want someone like that in your life? You're a goddamned hero, and if she can't see that, then you're better off without her."

"We have a child, Bates. It's not that easy."

"Get visitation rights. Val can watch her when you have her at the ranch."

Dane shook his head. "I'm not going to be that kind of father. My parents dumped me on my grandparents. I'm not going to dump my daughter on someone else to raise."

"Then you'd better take a good look at all your options. Find the one that is best for you. Then decide if playing daddy is your best shot."

Only the glow from the fireplace illuminated Dane's office. Lucky sat at his feet, content to chew on his elk antler. The crackling of the fire and the gnawing of Lucky's teeth were the only sounds that broke the silence. Dane nursed a glass of Chivas while staring at the chessboard in front of him. He usually found comfort in working on various chess moves. The game appealed to him by teaching patience and strategy. This time there was no comfort to be found. Instead, his conversation with Bates replayed in his mind.

He thought about what Bates had said to him. Bates knew Dane better than anyone, and yet to hear him say that Jules was not the right choice for him niggled at him. He trusted Bates. Bates had always called the shots, found the right angles, and kept Dane right on target. He'd never offered life advice and had never asked for it in return. Instead, Bates looked after Dane, especially after his accident. He was there to help him clean himself up when a seizure resulted in a bloodied head and the indignities of losing control of his bodily functions. Bates helped him without complaint or causing him embarrassment—something Dane appreciated.

Dane got to his feet, making his way to the fireplace. Taking the poker he jabbed at the extinguishing logs, stirring up the embers before he added another one to it. He should go to bed. It was late, and he knew that he had decisions to make before sleep would come to him. He stared into the fire, lost in thought.

He had a daughter. Dane let the word sink in. Daughter. He was a father. Not according to Red. His DNA didn't give him the right to call himself Becca's father. Deep down, he knew she was right because his father was nothing more than a DNA donor. His mother, too, if he was honest with himself. Dane closed his eyes, remembering the day when his parents drove him out to this house and left him with his grandparents. He was five years old. Old enough to know then that he was unwanted. He remembered his grandfather arguing with his father, although the words they exchanged Dane couldn't recall. Dane's grandmother held him in her arms. She was the one who cried while telling him everything would be alright as he stared at his mother who sat motionless in the passenger seat of the car. Dane would never forget the lack of emotion his mother showed, as though she was dropping off an unwanted pet at the pound and not her child.

When a child knows he's unloved and abandoned by his parents, the damage done can be everlasting. Fortunately for Dane, his grandparents gave him all of their love and more. They did their best to make him feel valued. Gramps taught Dane everything he knew about cattle ranching, shooting, and riding horses. Grams taught Dane how to cook, do laundry, and how to dance. *"Someday you'll want to sweep a woman off her feet, Dane, and dancing is the most romantic way to get to her heart, although knowing how to cook and clean will get you a gal, too."* Dane smiled, thinking of Friday nights with Gramps and Grams when they'd play their favorite music and Grams would take turns dancing with her two favorite men. They were long gone now, their ashes scattered on the ranch, and their names etched on a stone marker near the house.

Dane owed Becca more than what his parents gave to him. She deserved to know that she had a father who would adore her and keep her safe. She would never have to wonder why she wasn't good enough to love. How could he rationalize saving children around the world if he couldn't look after his daughter? Walking away was not an answer. Even if Jules refused to let him be a part of her life, Dane knew that he wouldn't let her keep him out of Becca's.

While in Afghanistan, Dane had spent days spread out flat on his belly, unmoving, his scope to his eye, waiting patiently for his target. If he could do that, to make his kill shot, surely he could wait for Jules to change her mind.

Chapter Seven

Two weeks had passed without any contact from Jules. Val left several messages on Jules' voicemail and even tried contacting her through the hospital. She wasn't surprised, although she couldn't hide the hurt she was feeling. Jules' anger had always been a force of nature that left many quaking in her path. It had always been wise to let Jules make the first move in restoring things to the way they once were. Jules had a loving and caring heart. Val and Ned knew that pediatrics would be the perfect fit for Jules. She had more patience for children than adults, and she was more forgiving, too.

During that time, Dane looked after business. The mission he had been asked to accept was taken care of—another success. It was a small rescue mission, quickly done by eight handpicked men. Although he ran everything from behind his desk, Dane never lost contact with his unit. It was a stressful time for him, and Val knew well enough to leave him alone. Dane would emerge from his office once he knew everyone, his men, and the people they rescued, were safe. Val made sure she had fresh homemade baking waiting for him along with a pot of strong coffee.

Jules looked up from her desk to find Dane standing in the doorway, holding a cardboard tray with two coffee cups and a small paper bag. Lucky stood beside him, wagging his tail.

"Val told me that Ned used to come in on Saturday mornings to clear up his paperwork. She said that you most likely would carry on the tradition." He nodded toward two empty chairs facing her desk. "Mind if we join you?"

Jules waved to the chairs. "Be my guest." She closed the file she was working on and added it to a stack on the end of her desk.

Dane placed the tray on the desk before taking off his coat and Stetson and piling them on one of the chairs. He took his seat before Lucky sat at his feet.

"The muffins are from Val. Banana walnut." Dane removed the lid from one of the coffee cups and offered it to Jules. "One cream."

"Thank you." Jules smiled before taking a sip of the hot beverage. "Did you garner how I like my coffee from Val's file? You know the one that you didn't look at?"

"If you must know, I didn't have to look at a file. You put cream in your coffee when you visited my ranch. I remember everything about you, Red."

"There's not much to remember."

Dane laughed. "You weren't a good liar then. You still aren't."

Dane took the lid off of his coffee and took a sip. He placed the cup on her desk, then sat back in his chair. He watched her, taking in everything about her. This morning Jules wore a dark blue turtle neck sweater under her white lab coat. Her name badge hung slightly crooked on the left lapel. She wore her red hair pulled back in a messy ponytail. Teddy bear earrings dangled from her earlobes.

"What are you staring at?" His gaze caused her to shift uncomfortably in her seat.

"You don't seem like the teddy bear earring type of woman."

Jules gave him a wry smile. "Why, Gary, I thought you said you knew me." Jules reached into one of her pockets and pulled out a stethoscope with red tubing and a teddy bear on the chest-piece. She placed it on the desk then pulled out an otoscope with the head of a panda, and ophthalmoscope with the head of a monkey. "Being in a hospital is stressful enough for a child. There's no harm in adding some fun to an examination."

Dane reached for the ophthalmoscope and looked through it. "I wonder if this monkey can see what's going on in my head." He placed it back on the desk.

"You don't know?"

"No one seems to know. I've had all the scans, all the tests. I've tried every drug—Topamax, phenobarbital, medical cannabis, and countless others. The side effects are worse than the problem. At least they are in my case." Dane gazed down at Lucky. "This guy has given me a new lease on life. I may not be able to control my seizures, but at least I don't fall flat on my face anymore. Too many scars and I'll scare the ladies off." Dane looked at Jules and winked.

"Have there been ladies to scare off?"

"Are you asking as Jules or Red?"

"Is there a difference?"

"Jules is in a relationship, whereas Red likes to play." He held her gaze, hoping she would say she was asking as Red.

She wouldn't take the bait. As much as she wanted to know if there had been other women in his life, her feelings were still raw when in his presence. She didn't want to know. Not yet.

"How's Val?"

"I think you know the answer to that question. Don't you think it's time to make peace with your aunt? Life is short, Jules. You and I both know how short it can be."

"I'm still mad."

"Over what? That she's working for me? She's an adult. She can do whatever she damned well wants to do."

"You don't get it. You never will."

"Maybe I won't, but I know that Val and Becca shouldn't be the ones you're punishing. You don't like what I do? Fine. I can live with that. Let Val back into your life. You came back here for her. Remember?"

Jules tore a piece off her muffin and put it in her mouth. She savored the taste. Jules had to admit that Val's baking was one of many things she missed where her aunt was concerned. Dane was right. Maybe it was time to move on and call a truce.

"I'm picking Becca up from daycare when I'm finished going through these files. Would you like to join us for lunch?"

"I'd like that. How long do you think you'll be?"

"About another hour. You can wait here if you'd like unless—"

"I can find something to do." Dane stood up. "We'll be back in one hour. Let's go, boy."

Dane headed out of the office with Lucky by his side. He pulled out his cell phone and made a call. "Hank, it's Dane Andrews. I'm at the hospital, and I've got an hour to kill. I know it's Saturday, but do you think you could swing by here? There's something I'd like to run by you." Dane pressed the call button for the elevator. "Thanks. I'm heading to your office now. See you soon. Hank? Let's keep this between us."

He arrived at her office door precisely one hour later. Jules tried not to stare at him. It was as though her eyes were no longer under her control. They roamed over his body, taking in every detail from the top of his perfect head of hair to the tip of his polished boot. The past five years hadn't aged him, only added a softness to his brown eyes that made her want to melt into them.

"Are you ready?" Dane asked, fully aware that she was ogling him.

"Just finished." Jules closed the last folder and added it to the pile.

Dane entered the office and made his way to the chair that held his coat and hat. While he put on his coat, he watched as Jules made herself ready. She released her hair from the messy ponytail and shook it free. Red hair fell in thick waves past her shoulders. She used her fingers to comb through her hair. Jules opened a desk drawer to fetch her purse. She opened it and pulled out her lipstick and applied the color to her lips without using a mirror. Dane marveled at her skill.

She caught him watching her. "Have you never seen a woman apply lipstick?"

"Not like that."

"I can do this with my eyes closed. During med school, my eyes were usually half-shut first thing in the morning. There was rarely the chance to look at a mirror. I'm sure there are things you can do with your eyes closed."

"Quite a few things." He knew she was playing with him, teasing him with double entendres. She was the Red he remembered from one night long ago when they used double entendres and knowing glances in a game that lasted for hours. "Where would you like to go for lunch?"

"Is your bar open?"

"Of course, it is."

"Does it have a children's menu?"

"We serve the best chicken fingers and fries in town."

"Then let's go there." Jules picked up her purse and moved toward the door. Her coat hung on the back of it.

"Allow me," Dane murmured as he removed the coat from the hook and held it for Jules to put on.

"Thank you."

They left her office walking side by side, with Lucky walking slightly ahead of Dane.

"Have you given any thought to what I said earlier? About Val?"

"Yes, and I've thought about you, too."

"And?"

"I've decided to call a truce. I may not like what you do, and it makes me angry thinking about it, but I want to get to know you. After all, you are Becca's father."

"Not just a DNA donor?"

"You're still in that category. There's room for improvement."

"What about Val?"

"I'll reach out to her. Soon."

Becca ran to Dane and Lucky when she caught sight of them standing with her mother at the entrance to the daycare. "Dane!" she called. "Lucky! I missed you."

"Dane's taking us out to lunch. Do you like that?"

"Yes!" Becca squirmed while Jules tried to put her jacket on her. "Can we have ice cream?"

"Don't you want to have lunch first?" Dane asked.

"After lunch, silly. Strawberry ice cream with oatmeal cookies."

"That's her favorite. Don't worry if your place doesn't serve it."

"What Becca wants, she will have." Dane took his cell phone out of his pocket and typed in a short message to Bates. "Do you have a car?"

"Yes. Why?"

"You're driving."

The Admiral's Eighth was busy for a Saturday afternoon. Dane knew it would be because of the Christmas shoppers visiting the downtown area. His bar allowed its patrons to relax in a comfortable environment, without music blaring, unlike many of the stores and restaurants in the neighborhood.

"Over here," Dane said as he pointed to a booth marked reserved.

They made their way toward it, Becca chattering excitedly. "Does Lucky have lunch, too?"

"He eats breakfast," Dane answered, happy to be in her company.

"Can he have dessert?"

"We'll see." Dane helped Becca with her coat then hung it on the hook outside their booth. "There you go," he said as he picked her up and sat her on the padded seat.

Jules took off her coat and hung it over top of Becca's, then took her seat beside her. Dane hung his coat over hers. He smiled, realizing that they had the appearance of being a family. He slid onto the bench across from them, followed by Lucky sitting at his feet.

Immediately, a waitress was at their table.

"Hi, there, welcome to the Admiral's. My name is Annie. I'm your server." She glanced at Dane, instantly recognizing him. "Boss. I didn't know this was your table." Her embarrassment betrayed her with a deepening blush.

"Hi, Annie. I'd like you to meet Becca and her mom, Jules. They're going to be regulars here."

"Hi," Becca said happily. "I want chicken fingers and fries, please."

"One of my favorites. How about the two of you? Do you know what you'd like to order? Or would you like to look at the menu?"

"What do you recommend, Dane?"

"We've got the best burgers in town."

"I'll have a burger with onion rings."

"Make that two," Dane said. "And two beer and one—"

"Milk is fine for Becca."

"Milk," he said before turning his attention to his table mates.

"Do you know what?" Becca asked, turning her attention to Dane.

"Tell me."

"Santa Claus will be here soon."

"He will?"

She nodded her head. "Yep, and he brings lots of presents for everybody."

"Yes, he does."

"We've been reading Christmas stories," Jules explained. "Becca is learning about Santa's workshop and his reindeer."

"Wow. How many reindeer does Santa have?"

Becca held up both hands with one thumb bent across her palm. "Nine!"

"Nine? I thought there are only eight."

Becca shook her head and laughed before she recited all of their names, "Comet, Cupid, Dasher, and Donner, and Dancer, Blitzen, and Prancer, and Vixen, and Rudolph in front!"

"Which one is Rudolph?"

"He's the one with the red nose, silly!"

"Right."

Their waitress, Annie, arrived with their drinks. "Your lunch is almost ready. I'll bring it to you shortly."

Dane thanked her, then turned his attention back to Becca. "Have you seen Santa and told him what you'd like for Christmas?"

The smile Becca gave him made his heart melt. "I want a doggie, and a pony, and more books."

"I told Becca that Santa couldn't bring a puppy with him on his sleigh. It's too long of a trip for a puppy. The same goes for a pony."

"You want a doggie? What kind?"

Becca needed no encouragement to talk about her dream dog. "He is white and brown, and he has long floppy ears."

"Like Flopsy?"

"Yep. And he has a long waggly tail. And he has short legs."

"Is it a Basset Hound?"

Becca shrugged her shoulders.

"Jules, do you know?"

"It could be. I don't know where she got the idea. Becca knows not to expect a lot of presents from Santa. He has all the children in the world to give presents to."

"Here you go," Annie announced when she arrived with their meals. "One chicken fingers with fries for Becca, and our burger special for Jules and Boss. Let me know if I can get you anything else."

"We're fine. Thank you," Jules said. She waited for Annie to be out of earshot before she whispered to Dane, "She calls you Boss."

He shrugged.

"Val calls you Boss, too. Why is that?"

Dane took a bite of his burger.

Jules wouldn't let him ignore the question. "Does everyone call you Boss? Is it your nickname?"

Dane swallowed then took a swig of his beer. "My unit called me Boss, and the name stayed with me."

"What does it mean?"

"It doesn't matter."

"It does to me. I want to know. Tell me."

"Not now."

"Why not?"

Dane glanced at Becca, who was busy eating her chicken fingers. His gaze returned to Jules, who hadn't touched her meal.

"Your burger's getting cold."

"I'm a mother. My food is always cold. Out with it."

"They call me Boss because when I was on a mission, I was in complete control. I took out the enemy without any of my men getting shot. We had the highest loss exchange ration of any unit."

"Loss exchange ratio?"

"Enemy kills."

Dane reached for her hand as he saw the color drain from her face. "Please, don't. Not here. Not now."

Jules pulled her hand away, recoiling from his touch.

"Why is Mommy white?"

"Mommy's not feeling well," Jules said quickly. "I'm sorry. I can't do this. We have to go, Becca."

"I'm not finished!"

"Red," Dane's voice was low and pleading. "Stay. Don't punish Becca."

"I'm not. We have to go. I'm not feeling well." Jules got to her feet. "Come on, Becca. It's time to go."

Dane stood up and motioned to Annie to come to their table.

"Yes, Boss?"

"They have to leave. Will you put their meals in a container? There's also a special dessert in the freezer for them. Bring that with you. Thanks."

"Sure thing. I'll be right back."

"We don't need to take our food with us."

"Yes, you do. Becca hasn't finished her lunch, and I promised her strawberry ice cream with oatmeal cookies. I don't break my promises. Ever."

He helped them with their coats.

Becca crouched down to talk to Lucky. "Bye-bye, Lucky. Too bad we couldn't have lunch with you. See you later."

"Here you go," Annie announced as she handed a thermal bag to Jules. "I hope you come back soon."

"Thank you," Jules replied. She turned to Dane. "Thank you for lunch. Goodbye."

Dane crouched to see eye to eye with Becca. "Goodbye, sweetie. Look after Mommy for me, okay?"

Becca wrapped her arms around Dane's neck and kissed his cheek. "Okay. Bye." She let go of him and took her mother's hand.

Dane stood up and watched Jules lead Becca out of the restaurant. He had never felt as powerless as he did at this moment. Red had cut him off at the knees because of a nickname. He was proud of that name. His men had given it to him, and he'd be damned if he let anyone make him feel ashamed because of it.

"What set her off this time?" Bates asked from behind Dane's back.

"My name. My fucking name."

At that moment, Lucky's wet nose pressed against the back of his hand. Dane looked down at his dog and shook his head. "You've got the damnedest timing, boy."

Chapter Eight

"This is it," Val Williams said to Bates as he neared the driveway to Jules' townhouse.

"You sure you don't need backup?" Bates looked at her in his rearview mirror. Val had been fidgeting during most of the drive—something that would have bothered him if he didn't have Boss on his mind.

"Don't joke about something like that. Jules invited me. I'll be fine. You can go and do whatever it is you do when you're in town."

He steered the vehicle into the driveway and turned off the ignition.

"What do you think I do?" Bates' furrowed brow betrayed his usually expressionless face.

"I have absolutely no idea. Maybe you have a lady friend you visit. Or perhaps you treat yourself to a spa day."

Bates stared back at her. "You don't want to be late." He opened his driver's door then stepped out of the SUV to make his way to the back passenger door.

Val waited for him, knowing how much he didn't like anyone to break the rules. She was aware of what he was doing without having to watch him. Bates took his time, surveying the area, looking for any possible threat, before he let her exit the safety of the vehicle. She knew she was safe. Dane had assured Val when she first joined his staff that Bates had some quirks that she would find odd. He told her to go with the flow, and not let him get to her. That's what Val did, and in return, she took liberty in teasing the man whenever she could.

Her door opened, and a hand reached in for her. She handed Bates a tote bag filled with Christmas baking and a few gifts. Jules' phone call a few days ago had given Val plenty of time to bake and purchase a few presents for her niece and grandniece.

"Thank you, Bates," she said as she exited the SUV.

They walked to the front door of the house.

"This walkway needs to be cleared properly. Someone could get hurt."

"No one clears a walkway like you."

"Damned right."

Val rang the doorbell. The sound of Becca's voice announcing to her mother that Auntie Val had arrived caused Val's heart to swell.

"Aunt Val," Jules said with a sigh of relief upon opening the door. "You came."

"You invited her, didn't you?" Bates accusatory tone surprised her.

"That's not—" Val shook her head. "Don't mind him. He's miffed that your walkway has some snow on it."

"Merry Christmas." Bates handed the tote bag to Val. "Call me when you're ready to leave. Boss and I will pick you up."

"Will do. Thank you, Bates."

Jules stepped back to allow Val entry. As soon as the door closed, they could hear the sound of a shovel clearing the walkway.

Jules gave Val a questioning look to which Val smiled and answered, "That's Bates. He has to have things done right."

Val shrugged off her coat and hung it on the antique coat rack by the front door. She slipped off her boots before following Jules into the living room.

"Today works out perfectly for our visit. Dane had plans for coming into town, so I hitched a ride."

"I didn't see him in the car with you."

"Bates dropped him off first. Dane didn't want to cause any problems. He said your last meeting didn't end on good terms."

"No, it didn't."

Val looked around the room. "This room looks like it did the last time you lived here. It didn't take you long to settle in again, did it?"

"Not when professionals put the house back together for me. I couldn't have done it with Becca underfoot."

Val placed the tote bag on the coffee table. "I brought you some Christmas baking, and—" she paused while she pulled out a Christmas stocking filled with presents. "This is for you. I remember how much you looked forward to your Christmas stocking first thing Christmas morning."

"Aunt Val, I—"

"Hide it somewhere then put it out beside Becca's on Christmas Eve. You have a stocking for Becca, don't you?"

"Of course I do. She's into Santa big time. Every night she crosses off the number of sleeps before he arrives."

"Speaking of Becca, where did she run off to?"

Jules put the stocking back in the tote bag. She pressed her finger to her lips and whispered, "She's discovered a new game, hide and seek. She wants you to find her."

Val smiled with amusement. "I haven't played that game in ages. Not since you were a little girl. Make sure there's a cup of coffee waiting for me after I find her. We can sample some of my baking if you like. I made your favorites. At least they were your favorite."

"If they're your shortbread cookies, they are still my favorite." She gave Val a warm smile. "You might want to look in my O F F I C E," she said, spelling out the word.

Val nodded in agreement, deciding first to pretend to look for Becca in the living room.

"Becca, where are you? Are you in the living room? Are you hiding under the tree?"

Val moved through the room, making loud sounds so that Becca would hear her. Eventually, she made her way to Jules' office and called out, "Is Becca in here? I wonder where she could be."

Val searched for the little girl, looking behind the curtains and the furniture. "No, she's not here," she announced. Val got to her hands and knees to look under the furniture. "Not here either. Where is she? Oh, I know," Val said happily. "She must be under Mommy's desk. Val made her way around the large antique desk, confident she would find Becca. The child was nowhere.

"Becca?"

With her hands on her hips, Val took a final look around the room. It was a large room. A love seat, two winged-back chairs, two large wooden bookshelves, and a massive and heavy antique desk fit nicely in it.

"Child, where are you?" Val huffed. She moved to the doorway and called out, "Jules! I can't find Becca."

Jules walked out of the kitchen, laughing at her aunt. "You can't find Becca?"

"I'm serious, Jules. If she's not in the office, where else would she hide?"

"I saw her go into the office myself." Jules ignored the slight stab of panic in her belly. "How hard is it to find a four-year-old?" she asked as she made her way into her office. "Becca! Where are you?"

"She has to be in another room," Val said, trying to reassure Jules.

"No." Jules shook her head. "She knows the rules. She doesn't go upstairs without me. There's only the main floor for hiding—living room, kitchen, the office, and the bathroom."

"Then I'll look for her on this floor, and you go upstairs just in case she decided to change the rules of the game."

"Becca!" both women called out.

Their search became desperate. Val heard the slamming of doors upstairs as Jules exited each checked room. The sound of Becca's name echoed throughout the house. She checked the living room, tossing cushions to the floor in case the child was hiding beneath them.

"Becca, this isn't funny. Please come out wherever you are. You won, sweetie. Auntie Val doesn't want to play anymore." She listened, hoping to hear the child's giggle, only to hear Jules' footsteps upstairs on the wood floor.

Val returned to the office. "Becca? The game's over. Please come out."

Jules made her way down the stairs.

"Did you find her?"

Val, unaware of Jules standing behind her, startled with a gasp. "No. Jules. I'm worried."

"Becca," Jules cried out.

Val walked to the foyer in search of her purse. She pulled out her cellphone and pressed the call button.

"Who are you calling?"

Val held up her finger to quiet Jules. "Bates, we can't find Becca. Please come and help us."

It wasn't until she heard the urgency in her aunt's voice that Jules allowed panic to take hold of her. She steadied herself against the staircase railing.

"She can't be gone, Val. Do you think she's been kidnapped?"

"No! What makes you think that? If anyone can help us find her, it's Dane and Bates. Do you think she could have slipped outside?"

"She can't open the door. It's too heavy for her. There's no way she could be outside."

"She's almost five, Jules. Don't underestimate her."

"This is all because of him, isn't it?"

"What? You can't possibly think that Dane had anything to do with this."

"You work for a man who has a personal bodyguard and lives in a high-security compound. He must have made a lot of enemies. Don't you think someone has taken Becca because of him?"

Val couldn't answer her niece. She had no explanation for Becca's disappearance, and she refused to let her imagination run away with her.

"Let's keep our wits about us, okay?" Val opened the front door and stepped onto the landing. "Becca!" she called out then cursed Bates for clearing off the walkway. There was no way to tell if little feet had stepped outside.

"Becca!" Jules called out from beside her. She grabbed Val's hand. "Where is she?"

Val heard the sound of a car racing down the street toward them. In seconds, the black SUV pulled up the driveway, and both the driver's and passenger doors opened.

"What's happened," Dane called out as he ran up the walkway with Lucky and Bates behind him.

"It's Becca," Val said, trying to stay calm. "We can't find her."

Bates turned and surveyed the area. There were no footprints in the snow. "Do you think she's outside?"

"No. She can't open the front door. It's too heavy for her."

"You don't think someone has—" Val couldn't say the words.

"She's gone because of you!" Jules lashed out at Dane.

Dane opened the front door. "Let's get inside."

They entered the house. Both Dane and Bates took in their surroundings. Dane nodded to Bates, who then proceeded to make his way up the stairs.

"Answer me! This is because of you, isn't it?"

Dane turned to face Jules and leveled her with a furious gaze, and yet his voice was calm. "No. This has nothing to do with me. Settle down and let's figure out where Becca is. Where did you see her last?"

"When I arrived," Val answered. "Jules and I walked into the living room. That's when I noticed Becca wasn't with us, and Jules said that Becca would be hiding."

"She likes to play hide and seek," Jules said, wiping at her tears. "I saw her go into my office. There's hardly anywhere to hide in there. That's why—" She stopped when Dane and Lucky headed for the office.

"I took my time finding her," Val explained. "I wanted her to think she was hard to find."

Dane held up his hand, motioning her to be quiet.

"Find," Dane ordered Lucky. "Find Becca."

Three weeks of yearning to be with his newfound daughter gave Dane plenty of time to focus his energy on her safety. He knew that Lucky was smart and talented. His knowledge of verbal commands was extraordinary. Although Lucky was trained to make Dane his sole responsibility, he had a fondness for Becca. Dane knew that the moment he awakened to find the little girl sitting beside the dog reading to him. Lucky didn't tolerate anyone in his space when he was working. Except for Becca. Dane worked with Lucky to keep Becca safe. It turned out that Flopsy wasn't the only thing left behind. Becca left behind a dirty T-shirt, and Dane made use of it by playing hide and seek with Lucky. Dane challenged the dog's sense of smell, and the dog never disappointed him. No matter where Dane hid Becca's shirt, Lucky found it.

His nose to the floor, Lucky ran to Jules' antique desk and sat. He didn't make a sound. The wagging of his tail was the only sign he gave.

"Good boy," Dane said as he kneeled beside his dog. "Bates," he called out.

"What's he found?" Jules asked.

"How long have you had this desk?" Dane asked as he examined its exterior.

"Since I bought this house. The original owners didn't want to take it with them because of its size, so I kept it. Why?"

"Becca?" Dane asked as he pulled on the drawers.

Both sides of the desk had three drawers all with locks. The three on the left side opened. The right side was different. None opened.

"Do you have keys for the desk?"

"No. I should have had the locks changed, but I never got around to it."

"You've never opened it? Not even by accident?"

"No! What is it?"

Bates arrived and made his way to the desk and crouched beside Dane.

"I can't find the latch. There has to be a trigger here."

"What do you think it is?" Bates asked him.

"I came across one in London in an antique store. This side here is a safety box. It opens by pressing a lever. They were made to protect valuables. There's a story about a man who put his child in one when his house came under attack."

"You think Becca's in it?"

Dane nodded. "The damned thing must be soundproofed. Otherwise, I'm sure she'd be letting us know she's inside."

The men moved their hands over the wooden drawers as they tried to feel the hidden lever.

"It's got to be at her eye level."

Lucky began to whine, his tail wagging excitedly.

"Easy boy," Dane said softly. "Damn it. If a child could find it, why can't we?"

Dane looked to Jules. "Does Becca ever sit with you at your desk? Or have you seen her sitting here by herself?"

Jules stood close to the desk. "She likes to open the middle drawer. She puts her bunny in it and pretends he's sleeping so that she can do her work."

Dane opened the middle desk drawer. There was no bunny. He emptied the contents onto the desk surface and then felt the inside of the drawer.

"Look underneath the desk. Jules used to play at her father's feet when she was a toddler. It's how he used to keep her busy when her mother needed some time to herself."

Jules took Val's hand in hers, thankful that her aunt was with her.

Bates pulled the chair away from the desk while Dane got to his knees and looked under the desk.

"Here," Bates said as he handed Dane a pocket flashlight he'd taken from inside his jacket.

Dane took the flashlight then rolled onto his back, pushing himself under the desk. He shone the light on the woodwork, and with his free hand, he felt the edges and surface of the wood, trying to find something that would act as a lever to open the desk.

"What the hell did you touch, sweetheart," he murmured as his keen eyes searched for a clue.

"Anything?" Bates asked.

"Nothing. Hold on. There's something—"

It was smaller than the size of a fifty cent coin, wooden, made out of the same material as the desk and stained to match the wood grain, inset in the right side. Dane pushed the circle and waited. Slowly, the wood side began to slide out from under the desk.

"It's opening," Bates said.

"Come on," Dane urged under his breath, impatient to see his Becca.

He kept the light aimed at the opening. Hopeful of finding her conscious.

"Dane, you found me!"

Becca's bright eyes and toothy smile greeted Dane. She lay on her side, cradling Flopsy.

"You found a perfect hiding place, sweetie."

"I did, didn't I?"

"Do you want to come out now?"

She nodded her head yes. Dane reached for her and pulled her out of her hideaway. He hugged her to his chest.

"I've missed you, little one."

"Silly, Dane!" Becca teased.

"Lucky's here. Why don't you go out and hug him? He's the one who found you first."

"Okay." Becca scrambled off Dane and made her way out from under the desk.

Dane wiped his hand over his face and let out a heavy breath.

"Lucky!"

Dane smiled at the sound of her voice. She had no idea the ordeal she had created. He imagined this would be a story for later. Much later.

"Becca!" Jules cried out.

"Don't," Val whispered, holding her hand tight. "Don't make a fuss. Look at her. She wasn't scared. Don't upset her."

Jules looked at Val and nodded. Val always kept a cool head about her. It was something Jules didn't fully appreciate until now.

"Why don't we make coffee? Auntie Val brought Christmas cookies for you and Mommy, Becca. Should we have some?"

"Yes!" she answered happily.

Dane examined the hiding place. He felt the base with the palm of his hand.

He whistled softly. "Amazing."

It was made to open with the pressing of the disk. Once the child or contents were placed on the base, and the weight settled, the sliding mechanism would cause the compartment to close and keep the contents hidden or, the disk could be pressed again to close it. Dane tried it a few times to make sure he was right.

"Are you done playing?" Bates asked dryly.

"Yes," Dane answered before sliding out from under the desk. "Fine piece of mechanics," he said when he got to his feet.

"We should burn it."

"No," Dane answered thoughtfully. "We know how it works, and Becca's not afraid of it. It stays. Agreed?"

Bates nodded. "Understood."

"We should talk," Val said to Jules as they made the preparations for coffee and cookies.

"Not now."

"I wasn't blind when I agreed to work for Dane. My eyes were opened wide, then more so once I got to know him."

"He's a gun for hire."

"He hasn't shot a gun since he had his accident."

"You know what I mean, Aunt Val."

Val stopped placing cookies on the plate and leaned against the edge of the countertop. She folded her arms across her chest. "Do you ever listen to the news?"

"Of course I do."

"Then you've heard of the atrocities that happen all over the world. Despots that torture and torment innocent lives without a second thought. Armies that kidnap children and turn them into child soldiers or sex slaves."

"I get it. There are evil people in the world. That doesn't excuse what he does."

"Dane travels to the places that are forgotten by the rest of the world. He saves innocent lives, Jules. He saves women and children condemned to a cruel and horrific life. He and his men, they're heroes. What they do—they do it without expecting any glory or recognition. You'll never see their names on a plaque or read about them in the paper."

"Bad things still happen, Aunt Val. I don't think what he does is working."

"I think things would be a lot worse in the world if it weren't for men like Dane."

"Let's agree to disagree, okay?"

"He deserves better from you."

"Why?"

"If I have to point it out to you—" Val sighed heavily. "Why do I even bother? You won't listen. You never do when you get stubborn like this. You'll just have to figure it out for yourself."

"Aunt Val, I don't want how I feel about Dane to come between us. I came home to High River for Becca to be with her family. You are all we have."

"I want us to be family, too, but I won't leave him to help you raise Becca."

Jules nodded her head in agreement. "I don't expect you to. I've enrolled her in the hospital's daycare."

"I'm sure she's made lots of friends."

"I wish I could remember all of their names. The stories she tells me when I bring her home—" Jules smiled as she thought of their conversations. "I don't know if they're make believe or real."

"She must get that from you. You were always good at making up stories. And from what I've gathered, that's what brought Becca into our lives."

"You're not going to let this drop are you?"

"Give him a chance, Jules. That's all I'm asking."

Jules chose to sit by Dane. There were other places to sit in her living room, on one of the armchairs, a stool by the fireplace, or on the cushions piled on the floor—Becca's favorite spot. Her choice was not lost on Val who busied herself listening to Becca read to her from a book of Christmas stories, or Dane, who got to his feet when she entered the room. Lucky raised his head to take note of everyone's whereabouts and then lay back down on the floor near Dane's feet. Bates had left the room, taking note of the townhouse's security system.

She offered Dane his refilled mug of coffee. "I'm sorry for what I said to you earlier."

"How earlier," Dane teased. "You've said quite a lot to me."

She nodded her head, the slight blush of embarrassment touched her cheeks. "I deserve that. I blamed you for Becca's disappearance. I'm sorry for jumping the gun."

The use of the word gun did not escape Dane. "Guns aren't meant to be jumped, Red. Don't you know how dangerous that can be?"

"How can you find this funny?"

"If I couldn't laugh at serious stuff, I'd go crazy." Dane took a sip of his coffee. "Maybe I am crazy." He gazed over at Becca. "I'm crazy about her."

"She'll make you crazier. I'm sure she gave me a few gray hairs today. No more playing that silly game."

Dane turned his gaze to Jules. "Let her play hide and seek. Let her inside the desk if she wants to. I'll show you how to open it."

"Why should I let her hide in the desk? It could have been her death trap."

"Becca wasn't afraid of being in it. She was confident someone was going to find her. You don't want her to think that she should have been afraid if you don't let her play in it again." Dane looked back at Becca. "Besides, it never hurts to have a safe place in case you need it."

Jules placed her hand on his arm. "What is it you're not telling me? Is there someone after you? Could we be in danger?"

Dane turned to her. "No one's in danger. I'm overly cautious. I've seen a lot of bad in the world. I can't help bringing some of it back with me."

"Val thinks of you as a hero."

Dane chuckled. "Hero? No. I did my job."

"Do you miss it? Being in action?"

Dane placed his mug on the coffee table before him. "There are different kinds of missing. I can still fire a gun, although I can't go on a mission. I miss being able to do that. Then there are the other things I miss, my simple pleasures, like riding my motorcycle, riding my horse, and driving. It took some getting used to having Bates drive me everywhere."

"Having a driver isn't so bad. I wouldn't mind one."

"Ask your aunt how she likes Bates as her chauffeur. Better yet, I'll give him to you for a week then you can tell me how lucky I am."

"You're war buddies."

"That doesn't even come close. We're each other's life safer. The number of times we've saved the other's butt." He shook his head and smiled. "We need each other, and neither one of us is too proud to admit it."

Jules glanced over at Val and Becca. They were why she came back to High River. She wanted Becca to know and love the woman who had helped raise her when her life had been shot to hell. There it was again, the gun reference. Jules sighed, realizing that she couldn't ignore guns, especially now.

"Why did you tell me about what you do? You could have kept it a secret. I'd have been happy with you being the owner of a bar."

"We don't have secrets, remember?"

"We could have. This one time."

"I don't lie. I never have."

"The night we met—"

"We played a game. We didn't lie to each other."

"You see everything in black and white."

"So do you. Don't deny it."

"I'm not. It's just that—"

"It's what?"

"I don't know what to think about you."

"So you want to think about me? That's good." Dane shifted his weight and leaned into the back of the sofa. "Thinking can be overrated. Go with your gut, Red. You did that the night we met. Do it again."

"I have Becca to think about now."

"We both have Becca to think about now."

Jules startled, realizing Bates stood in the doorway watching them. "Geez," she muttered. "Does he always do that? Just appear out of nowhere?"

"You'll get used to him." Dane nodded to Bates. "What's up?"

Bates motioned for Dane to join him.

"Excuse me," Dane said as he got to his feet.

Bates waited for Dane to get out of Jules' hearing range. "All the locks need to be upgraded. They're shit. The little one could open them if she put her mind to it."

"Do it. Anything else?"

"The backyard fence should be replaced once the snow is gone. It's not keeping anything out and it won't keep the mite in."

"Okay. What about cameras?"

Bates' eyebrow raised. "Spying?"

"No. Keeping them safe. I want cameras at the access points so that Jules knows who's at the door before she opens it."

"We'll get it done. Have you told her you're upgrading her security?"

"Not yet. I just told Jules she wasn't in any danger. She's not going to like this."

"What are you two whispering about?" Jules asked from behind Dane. She'd managed to approach the men without them noticing.

Dane cleared his throat as he turned to face her. "I asked Bates to check your locks on the house and windows. They need replacing. We can do that for you."

"I thought you said we weren't in any danger."

"Anyone could break in here. Robberies. Kidnapping," Bates offered.

"This is one of the safest neighborhoods in the city."

"You can't be too careful," Dane replied. "Do you mind letting us upgrade your locks? It's your house. Your call."

"If you think it's necessary, do it. And thank you."

"What for?"

"For finding Becca. I would never have thought—"

"It's okay."

The chime of the doorbell interrupted them.

"Expecting company?"

Bates, closest to the door, opened it, using his body as a protective barrier between the visitor and the people in the house.

"What do you want?"

"I'm Dr. Mark Blackwell. I'm here to see Dr. Jules Montgomery. Who are you?"

"Mark!" Jules gasped, her hand covering her mouth. "I forgot!"

"Forgot what?" Dane asked as he watched Jules push by him and then Bates.

"Mark! I'm so sorry. Come in. Please. I forgot about our plans."

Jules looked over her shoulder at Bates. "Let him in."

Bates stood back without taking his eyes off the man.

Mark stepped into the house and glanced around him, noticing that the two large men stood with arms crossed as though they were Jules' personal security team.

"Jules? What's going on?"

"We brought Val over for a visit and then decided to stay for coffee," Dane answered for Jules. "Jules forgot to tell us she invited anyone else."

"Mark volunteered to take Becca and me to the hospital daycare's Christmas party."

"Do you have your Christmas cookies? You told me you have a great recipe for shortbread."

Jules felt the heat from her reddening cheeks. Embarrassed by how easily she blushed made her blush deepen.

She startled when Val answered for her. Val stood in the entrance-way to the living room, carrying Becca on her hip. "The cookies are made and ready to go. Why don't we take Becca upstairs and get the two of you ready?"

"Are we going to a party?" Becca asked as they started up the stairs.

"Yes, sweetheart, and I think there may be a surprise visitor at the party."

"Dane? Is Dane coming?"

"No, Dane's not coming. Mark is taking you and Mommy."

"Oh, okay." Her disappointment was made clear to everyone, especially Dane.

Mark shifted on his feet, uncomfortable under the watchful eyes of the two men before him. After a few moments, the awkward silence became unbearable.

"It's just a party for the kids," he blurted out. "They'll have some treats, and then Santa will drop by and give them a present. I'll have them home in a few hours."

"Define a few," Dane's voice was low and threatening.

"It's over by six. We'll be back here no later than six-thirty. Is that okay with you?"

"Is what okay with them?" Jules asked as she descended the stairs.

Mark's head shot up to see her. Instant relief crossed his face. "They wanted to know when you'd be returning home."

"Are you planning to house sit while we're out?"

"Just having a friendly conversation," Dane answered, his gaze still fixed on the man in front of him. The man who would be spending the next few hours with his daughter and enjoying her delight in being at a party, having treats, and seeing Santa. At that moment he hated Mark Blackwell with every fiber in his being.

"We're ready," Val announced as she descended the stairs with Becca holding her hand.

Becca smiled broadly, proud of the pretty Christmas party dress her mother had purchased for her. It was a sparkly green princess dress, perfect for a four almost-five-year-old who believed in fairy tales and fairy princesses. Flopsy wore a sparkly green bow tie around his neck.

"You're beautiful," Dane gushed. His gaze took in Jules. "Both of you are stunning."

Jules wore a green dress, too. Not glittering like Becca's, but a deep Christmas green that hugged her curves in all of the right places—a dress similar to the one she wore when she first appeared in his life. When she asked him to play a game, and he agreed.

"We should be going." Mark's announcement pierced the bubble around them.

"Yes. We should leave, too. Val? Do you have everything?"

"My bag's in the kitchen. Give me a second."

"Will you help Becca with her coat, Dane?"

"Sure." Dane took the coat off the coat rack and crouched to help the little girl with her coat. "You're going to be the prettiest princess there. I hope you have lots of fun."

She nodded her head and smiled.

Dane took their coats from the rack, handing Bate's his then putting on his.

"Val!"

"Coming," she called out as she made her way from the kitchen. "Have a wonderful time," she said as she kissed Jules' cheek. "And you, little missy, you have fun, too."

Dane helped Val with her coat.

Bates opened the front door. "Let's go."

Dane held out his hand to Mark. "Goodnight, Doctor."

"Goodnight."

"Lucky. Home." Dane exited the house with his dog at his side.

He opened the rear door of the SUV and nodded for the dog to jump in. He followed, leaving Bates to look after Val. Once they were all settled in the vehicle, before the winter's chill had left the interior of the SUV, a colder voice broke through the silence.

"Let's get the hell out of here."

Dane leaned his head against the headrest and closed his eyes. He should be the one taking his daughter to see Santa, not some stranger. It tore at his insides, knowing that she didn't realize that Dane was her father and that she could ask him to take her places and he would because that was what fathers were supposed to do.

Lucky's paw pressed against Dane's thigh. He whimpered as his nose pushed into the back of Dane's hand, the cold, wet nose warning him of an imminent seizure.

Dane cursed as he gazed down at his dog. "Now?"

Dane unbuckled his seat belt and spread out along the seat. One leg bent at the knee, with his foot flat on the floor while the other leg stretched out with the sole of his boot pressed against the door. Once settled, Lucky jumped onto him, laying on his torso, his head resting under Dane's chin.

"You okay, Boss?"

"Keep your eyes on the road, Bates. Get us home."

Chapter Nine

Dane regained consciousness in the back seat of the SUV, immediately aware of the eighty-five-pound weight on his chest that was licking his face.

"Good boy," he murmured, his hand rubbing the top of Lucky's head.

"You okay?" Bates' gruff voice reminded him that he wasn't alone.

"Feel like a truck hit me. Again."

"You were out for a long time, Boss. Val's come out a couple of times to check on you. We were going to head out to the hospital if you hadn't come to in a few minutes. You sure you're okay?"

"Just let me get inside the house." He groaned as he tried to move under his dog's weight. "Off!" Lucky didn't move except to secure his position on top of his master. "Off," Dane repeated.

"Want me to pull him off you?" Bates offered as he reached back for the dog's collar.

Lucky shifted his weight on Dane, moving closer to the back of the seat. He warned Bates off with a low growl.

"Shit. He won't let me near you. The dog's never done that before."

Dane, too tired to wrestle with his dog, relaxed beneath him. "Give him a minute. Let him settle down." His large hand stroked the dog's head. "Good boy. Good—"

He was out again. Bates had never seen this happen before. It had always been one seizure, and then Dane was conscious and tired, but able to get to his feet and carry on. Something was wrong.

He reached for his cellphone and pressed the dial button.

"Bates?"

"Get to the car now. I'm taking Boss to the hospital." He looked at his watch. "One minute then I'm leaving without you."

"I'm on my way."

Val arrived at the SUV with seconds to spare. Bates stood by the front passenger door, waiting for her.

"I could have opened the door myself."

"Don't argue."

Val slid onto her seat, looking at Dane unconscious on the back seat. She heard the slam of her door, and then Bates took his place behind the steering wheel. In seconds they exited the garage and sped down the laneway to the main road.

"What happened?" Val asked, feeling it was now safe to talk to Bates.

"He came to then went out again. The damned dog knew it. Wouldn't let me pull him off Boss."

"That's not like Lucky."

"It's not like Boss either. He doesn't have seizures back to back. Something's wrong. Very wrong."

The sound of Lucky whimpering, while he lay on top of Dane's body, brought tears to Val's eyes.

"We can't lose him, Bates. Not now."

Bates glanced at her. "There's never a good time to lose him."

Bates arrived at the hospital in record speed, pulling up to the Emergency entrance with his horn blaring, demanding immediate attention.

Val got out of the car and opened the rear passenger door. "Lucky, come here, boy."

The dog refused to move, answering Val with a sharp bark. For the first time, Val witnessed the hair on the dog's back rise, and she feared him.

"Here, boy. Off!"

Her commands were unheeded.

Bates opened the other rear door, and the dog barked at him, this time more threatening.

"You have to get the dog off him," an attendant ordered Bates.

"Don't you think I know that?"

Bates reached inside his jacket pocket and pulled out his gun.

"Don't you dare!" Val screamed.

"I have to. There's no other choice."

"Wait!" Val reached into her coat pocket for her cell phone. She pressed the call button.

"We haven't got time!" Bates yelled out.

Val looked across the rear seat. Her eyes locked with Bates, demanding that he listen to her. "Boss will never forgive you if you shoot his dog. We have to try Jules. Where are you? It's Dane. We're at the Emergency entrance. Bring Becca. We need her. Hurry!"

"What is it?" Mark whispered in her ear. "You've turned white as a sheet."

"It's Dane. Val needs us in Emergency." Jules didn't wait for Mark to speak. Hurriedly, she scooped up Becca and carried her out of the daycare.

Mark rushed after her. "Wait! What about her presents?"

"Deal with it!"

The visual of two redheads dressed in beautiful green dresses was a sight to behold. People stopped and stared as Jules raced down the corridor to the Emergency Department with Becca in her arms.

"What's wrong, Mommy?"

"Dane needs us."

"Is he sleeping?"

"I don't know, sweetie."

"He'll be okay. Lucky will keep him safe."

Various scenarios raced through Jules' mind as she ran with Becca. Was Dane shot? Did he lie to her, and his life was in danger? Was he in an accident? Was it a seizure? Jules hugged Becca tighter. They arrived at the entrance and witnessed the commotion occurring outside. Flashing colored lights lit up the pavement, and a crowd of people gathered around a black SUV.

Jules pushed her way through the crowd while holding onto Becca. "Let me through. I'm a doctor."

"Jules!"

"Aunt Val! What happened?"

"It's Dane. He's having seizures. Lucky won't let us help. We can't get near him."

"What can I do?"

"Not you. Becca. The dog adores her. Maybe she can coax him out of the car. Get him to move off Dane. We have to try or else—"

Jules heard the dog barking. His threatening bark terrified her.

"I don't know."

"They're going to shoot him if we don't get him out of there. Becca's our only chance. We have to try. Have Becca call the dog. See if he'll come to her. That's all I'm asking."

"She's not going near him."

"She doesn't have to. Have her call Lucky. Please."

"Becca? Will you call Lucky? He won't leave Dane, and we need him to. Can you call him and see if he comes to you?"

Becca smiled. "Lucky's my friend. He found Flopsy. He found me."

"That's right, sweetheart. Call him for Mommy."

Jules approached the SUV, wary of what Becca might see.

"Call him, Becca."

"Lucky!" she called out sweetly. "Lucky, come!"

The dog answered with a whimper.

"Lucky!"

Jules edged closer to the door.

Becca called out once more, "Come, Lucky."

Bates stood ready. His gun aimed at the dog. One wrong move and Bates would be forced to shoot him.

"His tail's wagging. He sees me, Mommy."

"Don't go any closer," Bates warned.

"This isn't working. Someone shoot the dog!" A voice yelled out from the crowd.

Jules inched closer to the SUV while Becca strained to get closer to Lucky, reaching for him.

"Down, Mommy. Put me down!"

Jules glanced at Bates.

He shook his head, "I can't let you get any closer."

"It's not safe, Becca. Call Lucky. Please."

"Lucky. Don't be scared."

The dog whined.

"Off, Lucky. Off!"

The dog turned his head to Dane and licked his face then jumped to the floor of the vehicle.

"Come, Lucky!"

The dog bounded out of the SUV toward Jules.

"Sit."

Lucky sat at Jules' feet.

"Good boy, Lucky. Let me down, Mommy. Lucky needs a hug."

Jules hesitated.

"Mommy!"

Jules relented, setting her daughter on her feet.

Immediately, the little girl's arms wrapped around his neck. "Good boy, Lucky. Don't be scared. Your daddy's going to be fine."

"How is he, Doctor?"

Dr. Burns glanced up from Dane's bedside. She recognized Jules from Dane's description of her when he came out of his coma after his accident five years ago.

"You're Red, aren't you?" She got to her feet.

"Jules Montgomery. I'm the new head of Pediatrics." She offered the doctor a cup of coffee. "I thought you might want one. And yes, I'm Red."

Dr. Burns took the cup of coffee and smiled appreciatively. "Perfect timing. Thank you." She motioned to an empty chair in the room. "Why don't you pull up a chair and we can have a chat."

Jules was happy to have the invitation. She brought the chair to Dane's bedside and sat next to the doctor.

"We've managed to stop the seizures for now. I'll be damned if I know what's brought this on. He's never had non-stop seizures."

Jules noticed the labels on the IV bags hooked up to Dane. "You're inducing a coma?"

"To calm his brain. We're monitoring his brain activity for now. I'm waiting for the results from his scans."

"What do you think caused it?"

"I don't want to hazard a guess. But, to be honest, I'd like there to be something, something that we can treat and stop the seizures altogether. Boss needs to get back to living his life the way he is meant to do. This living in limbo isn't him. It's not the Boss I know."

"You call him Boss, too."

Doc Burns smiled. "Force of habit. We all called him that. Still do. He saved our lives countless times."

"Do you mind telling me about him?"

"Not at all. What would you like to know?"

"Did he enjoy killing?"

"You get right to the point, don't you?"

"My parents died at the hands of a gunman, so you can understand why I ask the question."

"I'm sorry about that." Doc took a sip of her coffee. "So you know that he was in Special Elite."

"Yes. I know he was a sniper and holds a record for kills. And when he left the Navy, he took on jobs for the government to kill bad people. That's what he called them."

"He didn't enjoy killing. Boss excelled at firing a gun and hitting his target, and that ability allowed him to protect the good and kill the bad. That's how he looked at it."

"Didn't it bother him?"

"Not that any of us could tell. He always remained cool-headed and kept his optimism. He greeted every morning with a smile. I can't say the same about Bates."

"What happened to him?"

"Nothing happened to him in the physical sense. He was one of the lucky ones—never got hit, no scars except for the one Boss gave him during a training exercise. Boss nicked Bates with his knife when he wasn't paying attention. Bates—" Doc hesitated, looking for the right words to describe the man who meant the world to her. "He saw first hand what evil the bad could do. Like many of our soldiers, he was deeply affected by what he experienced. He brought it home with him and found it difficult to fit in. That's one of the reasons why Boss took him under his wing and hired Bates to work with him. Boss keeps Bates centered, and Bates keeps Boss safe, or as safe as he can. That damned dog is Boss's new protector."

"He's quite the dog. My daughter adores him."

Doc looked at Dane and then back at Jules. "Don't you mean yours and Dane's? He told me about Becca shortly after he found out he was a dad."

"Sharing DNA doesn't make him a father."

Doc choked, almost spilling her coffee. "What do you have against the man? Look at him! I realize he doesn't have the most handsome mug in the world, but that smile and those eyes, when they're open, can charm the pants off any warm-blooded female."

"Sex appeal—"

"I haven't finished. He has the kindest heart of any man I know. And he's loyal, as loyal as his dog. Once you have his trust, he'd do anything for you. And I mean anything."

"I know that."

"Then what do you have against him?"

"What if he's not as perfect as I remember him?"

Doc leaned back in her chair. "How perfect was he?"

"Toe-curling perfect."

"Damn."

A cacophony of voices filled his pounding head. Dane rolled his head in his pillow, trying to find some escape from the noise. If they'd only shut up so that the pain in his head could ease.

"Welcome back, pretty boy. You've got visitors."

He knew that smart-ass tone, and he recognized the scent of her perfume. In all the years he'd known her neither had changed. Dane would never admit it to anyone, but waking in the presence of Doc Burns reassured him that he was going to live another day.

One eye opened.

"That's good. Now open the other."

"What if I don't want to?"

"Then you'll miss out on two lovely ladies waiting to see that you're not brain dead. And I swear I'll give you that diagnosis if you don't want to see these two."

Dane opened his other eye. He blinked, trying to focus his vision. He looked around him, only seeing Doc Burns standing by his bed.

"Liar."

"They're here. The little one had to go pee. Mommy's a real looker."

"She's doesn't play on your team, Doc."

"So I gather, Daddy."

"How long have I been out?"

"Long enough for Jules and me to get to know each other. Now let me check you over before they return."

Doc Burns checked Dane's pupils with a penlight. "Follow my finger."

Dane obeyed.

"How's the head?"

"Hurts like hell."

"Hurts like hell normal or worse?"

"Normal."

"Good. Do you remember what happened?"

Dane shook his head. "Nothing." He glanced at the intravenous lines hooked up to his arm. "What are you giving me?"

"Drugs."

"One of your secret concoctions?"

"Yes. Let me know if it works."

"How will I know?"

"You don't die."

"Your bedside humor sucks, Doc."

"Ya, well fire me if you want."

Dane closed his eyes and felt himself falling into the comfort of the pillow.

"Stay with me, Master Corporal."

"I'm here. How long have I been out?"

"We put you into an induced coma to get that brain of yours to settle. You've been out for forty-eight hours. You seem stable now."

"Do you know what caused the seizures?"

"We're looking into it."

"What's that supposed to mean?"

"We found something."

There was a light tap at the door before Jules' head peeked around the corner.

"Is it alright to come in for a visit? I have two very excited redheads waiting to see you."

Doc waved them in. She turned to Dane. "We'll talk later."

"Dane!" The excited squeals of the four almost-five-year-old filled the room as she ran to his bedside.

Lucky wagged his tail, doing his happy dance for Dane. He pulled at the leash to get to Dane. Jules let him go, and in one leap, Lucky landed on top of his master.

"Hey, boy. Did you miss me?" Dane lifted his chin, trying to avoid the licks. Lucky wouldn't let him. "Okay, that's enough. Settle down, boy. Settle."

"Off!" Becca's little voice stopped the dog.

He jumped off the bed and sat beside Becca.

Dane smiled, amused. "Looks like Lucky has a new master." He reached for Becca. "Come here, little one."

"Careful," Doc warned. "Your IV."

"I'm okay." Dane picked up Becca and sat her beside him. "Have you been looking after Lucky for me?"

She nodded her head.

"He hasn't left her side," Jules said softly. "It's as though he's taken over as her guard dog."

Dane's gaze darted to her. "He's supposed to."

"He's your dog, Dane."

"I think this is my cue to leave. Master Corporal, we'll talk later. Jules, don't let him order you around. Let him know who's the real boss. Goodbye, Becca. Take care of Lucky, okay?"

"Okay."

Jules moved toward the bed, then sat on the chair close to it.

"Why does she call you Master Corporal?"

"It's her fallback. Whenever she's stressed or in a group, she calls me by my rank. You should hear what she calls me when we're alone."

"No, thanks. The two of you are close." Jules looked down at her hands, embarrassed by the feeling of jealousy she felt working its way into her.

"Yes, we are. It was Bates, Doc, and me for four tours of duty. We grew close. We still are."

Dane reached for Jules' hand. "Hey, why the sad face?"

"You scared Mommy," Becca's sweet voice answered for Jules.

"I did? I didn't mean to."

"It looks like little ears have been listening again."

"Why was Mommy scared?"

"Dane, don't—"

"Do you know why?"

"She said she couldn't lose you again. Silly Mommy. You weren't lost."

Dane gazed up at Jules. "You're not going to lose me, Red. I plan on sticking around for a very long time. I'll be here for Becca, and you no matter what. You're with Blackwell. Becca seems to like him."

"I'm not—" Jules felt the blush come to her cheeks and cursed the uncontrollable giveaway. It was best to deflect and not have to think about Dane and his admission. "What did Doc tell you? Do you know what's wrong with you?"

"I'm fine. Just a big guy with a crazy brain." He gave her his boyish wink.

"It's not funny. You scared the hell out of all us. Lucky went crazy."

"Bates wanted to shoot him," Becca piped in.

"What?" Dane pushed himself into a sitting position. "Why would he want to do that?"

"Becca? Remember what we talked about?"

"Oh, I forgot."

"Too late now. What did I miss?"

"Lucky was in protective overload. He wouldn't get off you, and he wouldn't let anyone near you. Bates tried, and Lucky lunged at him. Bates thought he'd have to shoot him."

"How did you get him off me?"

"It was Val's idea to use Becca. She knew how Lucky reacted to her. I thought she was crazy."

"I told him to get off you, and he did."

"You told Lucky to get off me? And he listened to you?"

Becca nodded her head. "I said, 'Off, Lucky' and he did."

"Son of a gun. It worked."

"What do you mean?"

"Lucky knows his family."

Jules had left with Becca to return her to daycare, leaving Dane alone with his thoughts and his dog.

Dane rubbed Lucky's head. "Good job, boy. You did great."

He knew the rules about service dogs—that they were to serve one master. Any deviation would confuse the dog, and it would not carry out its duties, most likely to the detriment of the one whose life depended on him. Lucky was different. Dane realized from the moment he met this dog that he was intelligent and capable of learning more than detecting Dane's seizures.

When Becca came into their lives, Dane knew that Lucky could do more, and he wanted him to do more. Dane rarely thought about the possibility of not surviving a seizure. He was of the firm belief that when it was his time to leave this earth, it was his time. However, with Becca in the picture, and the possibility that she would be spending time with him, Dane wanted to ensure her safety if he blacked out when alone with Becca. Her safety was paramount. He could go into the darkness, knowing that Lucky would protect her.

Dane was tired to the bone, wanting to sleep and yet sleep evaded him. He wanted to go home, listen to Kenny G or watch football, and enjoy one of his favorite bottles of scotch. Lucky would sit at his feet. Becca would be with him, too, reading one of her fairy tales to him. And Jules, she'd be sitting by his side, her body leaning against him and holding his hand. He wanted so much and now—

A hard rap on his door brought him back to the present.

"Bates."

"Doc said you could have visitors."

"I was wondering when you'd drop by."

Bates took the chair by Dane's bedside then gripped Dane's hand.

"You're okay?"

"I'm fine. I hear you and Lucky butted heads."

"Stubborn-assed dog. Just like his owner."

Bates released Dane's hand.

"Glad you didn't have to shoot him."

"Who told you?"

"Little ears, Bates." Dane gave out a heavy sigh. "It would have hurt like hell to lose this guy, but I would have understood."

"You would have been the only one. Your mutt's got a fan club. Val still won't let it go."

"How is she?"

"Baking up a storm. Making all your favorites for when you return. Know when that's going to be?"

"It can't be soon enough as far as I'm concerned. Doc wants to run a few more tests before I can come home."

"What kind of tests?"

"I don't know. She wouldn't say."

"Want me to go pay her a visit?"

Dane smiled, appreciating his concern. "She found something. That's all I can tell you."

Chapter Ten

Jules noticed Bates standing at the nurses' station outside of Dane's hospital room. She hoped to talk to the man who knew Dane the best even though Bates put her on edge. It wasn't his size, although she had to admit that he was intimidating the way he could fill a doorway or how he looked at her as though he were deciding if she was friend or foe. She felt like the enemy when around him. It was the way he could move, despite his size, quietly and quickly, and how he entered a room without her hearing a sound. He unnerved her. That's what it was. Bates got on Jules' nerves.

He glanced her way, for a brief moment, assessed her, then continued his conversation with the nurse. When he finished, Bates turned his attention to Jules who by this time, stood outside Dane's door looking in at him through the glass pane. He made his way to Jules, stopping behind her.

"He's out for the count. Doc gave him another sedative."

Jules jumped. "Damn it!" She turned to face Bates. "Do you have to sneak up on people?"

"You knew I was here."

"You were over there," Jules sputtered as she pointed to the nurses' station. She felt the burn of her blush and became angrier at her embarrassment. "I didn't hear you behind me!"

"Want me to wear a bell or something?" A thin smile broke through on his stony face.

"Isn't that against Special Ops rules?"

"Special Elite. But for you, I might have to make the exception."

"Why's that?"

Bates nodded toward the sleeping figure in the bed. "Boss's orders. I'm not to creep you out."

"He said that?"

"More or less."

"Do you ever call him by his name?"

"His name's Boss as far as I'm concerned. I hear you have a problem with it."

"I prefer Dane."

Bates grunted.

"Can we talk?"

"Aren't we doing that?"

"In private. My office."

Bates shrugged and started down the hall.

"Where are you going?"

"Your office."

"How do you—"

Bates stopped and turned to face her. "I know everything about you, doctor. You left your office door unlocked. Always lock it when you leave. You don't want strangers going through your things."

Jules barely kept her jaw from hitting the floor. This man was going to be her undoing. How could he know everything about her? And her office? What gave him the right to be in her office? When she had the chance, she was going to tell Dane that his sidekick still gave her the creeps.

Jules took in a calming breath. She would not let this man get to her. She needed answers from him, and going full-blown redhead ballistic on him would not help her in any way, although it sure as hell would make her feel better.

Bates led the way. He stopped outside the doorway, making room for her to enter.

"Thank you," she murmured as she passed by him.

Jules took her seat behind her large desk while Bates closed the door behind him. He sat in an armchair, his gaze never leaving her.

She returned his gaze and wondered what he was thinking. There were no tell signs, no glimmer in his blue eyes. They were an icy blue, cold as if reflecting the man inside.

"Why did you keep my identity from Dane?"

"Straight to the point. I like that."

"You don't strike me as a man who likes to play games."

"Not with women."

Jules didn't want to go down this path. She needed to ask him about Dane, and then she wanted him out of her office.

"So? Why did you keep my identity from Dane?"

"He wasn't ready for you. The man was a mess, still is in some ways. Adding you to the equation didn't seem right for either of you."

"How was he a mess?"

"Nope. Not going there."

"Why not?"

"Because he's allowed to have his secrets. His aren't mine to tell. If you want to know, ask him."

Jules leaned forward, resting her elbows on her desk. Her gaze searched Bates' face for a hint of empathy. "He's Becca's father. Why would you keep him from his daughter?" She waited for an answer then groaned her frustration at his lack of response. "He saves children all over the world! Why would he not want to know about Becca!"

"I never said he wouldn't want to know about you or Becca."

"You're playing word games with me, Bates. Please tell me the truth."

Bates reached into the inside pocket of his jacket. He pulled out four prescription bottles and set each one on the desk. "These are mine. I need these to get me through every single day. I didn't get my bell rung by a tractor-trailer like Boss. Some days I wish I could trade places with him, so he doesn't have to suffer the way he does."

"PTSD—"

"Don't!" Bates held up his hand to stop her. "I'm not talking about me. I'm talking about Boss. You're a doctor. You should know that drugs made to cure us can also kill us. Drugs don't work for him. Every damned side effect you could imagine, he suffered. Did you know that suicide is one of the side effects of most of the drugs Doc prescribed him? We were lucky to notice the signs and get him off the shit before he killed himself. It was Doc who found Lucky. If it weren't for that dog, Boss would be six feet under by now."

"Val calls Lucky Dane's lifesaver."

"She's right about that. We were getting Boss sorted out when he decided to hire a housekeeper. Val was the best candidate, and when I discovered that you were part of her family, I decided to keep you a secret. He wasn't ready to bring anyone into his life, especially you or a child."

"I could have helped him."

Bates laughed without humor. "Don't kid yourself, doctor. You would have treated him the same way you're treating him now—with contempt and hatred."

"I don't hate him." Jules felt the burn come to her cheeks, angered by his accusations.

"You hate what he does, and it's the same thing. If you can't accept all of him, you're not any good to him. Boss has his pride. The last thing he needs is a woman who tries to make him feel guilty about what he does, especially when there's a helluva lot of people who are alive because of him."

"I know that he's a good man."

"But?"

"It's the guns. I can't accept them."

"Don't hate the man because you hate guns."

"I'm trying not to."

"Try harder, doctor, or get the hell out of his life." Bates stood and leaned across Jules' desk. His palms pressed flat against the surface as his face came within inches of Jules' face. "That night when you asked him to protect you from that creep Sinclair, Boss didn't know you from Eve. He went against every rule he made for himself by playing a game you started. He kept you safe, out of harm's way while he let me deal with Sinclair."

"You were the one? John could have died!" Jules stared into the blue eyes that seemed to grow colder with each second she held his gaze.

"You could have, too, if we hadn't stepped in to help you."

"I don't believe you."

Bates straightened then stepped back from the desk. He reached into his jacket and pulled out an envelope. He placed it on her desk. "Have a look at this then decide who is worse, Dane Andrews or John Sinclair."

Chapter Eleven

She held his hand and watched the rise and fall of his chest as he lay sleeping. Jules didn't want to wake Dane. She wasn't ready to talk to him. Instead, she sat by his bedside and thought about the man who represented everything she hated. She'd tried finding out whatever she could about him on the internet. There was very little to be found, only a blurb about the Canadian sniper, known as Boss, who was famous for his number of kills and the record-breaking long-distance shot that took out a wanted terrorist. He lived a secret life. His ranch outside of High River was evidence of that.

Aunt Val and Doc Burns adored Dane. He was their hero, and there was no arguing with them on that point. Neither of them could understand why Jules found it hard to accept Dane for the man that he was. They were right. He was a hero. He had been her hero once.

For one night she had asked him to play the part of Gary, a bush firefighter who was in town to spend the weekend with her. And he did willingly. This handsome stranger fell into the game quickly, playing the role of the loving boyfriend. He was perfect. He knew all the right things to say. He knew how to dance, and he knew how to make her laugh and forget that another man had threatened her. He could make up stories about their time together, and she believed him, adding her fantasies to their game.

Jules remembered how she felt. She felt loved, desired, and safe, even though she knew it was only for that night. A one time experience with a man who Jules knew deep down in her soul could be the one, and yet she knew that the timing was all wrong. She had made plans to move to Toronto and take a position at one of the world's leading hospitals. She had dreams, and none of them included High River.

Jules was afraid that in the morning light, she would find that she had woken up with a fairy tale frog or worse and that her fantasy man was a big mistake. Instead, he was asleep next to her, still the handsome prince. She kissed him goodbye before leaving his bed.

Dane told her that they knew more about each other from that one night than most couples did in a lifetime together. Although she tried to argue with him, she knew that he was right. They had a connection that was more than a physical attraction. They got each other.

Jules smiled as she remembered him testing her to find out if she was a quick-tempered redhead when he questioned her choice in men.

"If I'm going to be playing the role of your dream man, don't you think I should know what you expect of me? I need more than bush fire-fighter with broad shoulders. Unless you don't have much imagination or expect much from the men in your life."

"Are you suggesting I'm inexperienced or have bad taste in men?" Her cheeks burned red as she got up from their table.

"So, it is true. Redheads do have a temper."

She felt her cheeks burn as she thought of how he teased her. She did have a temper, and she had taken it out on Dane more than once. She sighed, remembering how she accused Dane's occupation as being the reason why Becca had disappeared when it was that antique desk that had been the culprit. And when she first found out who he was? She still felt embarrassed over her reaction. She was right to be upset, but in retrospect, she did overreact. She always went too far, and she always got away with it. No one had ever stood up to her temper. No one except for Dane. With everything she threw at him, he answered her with a calm voice and a twinkle in his eye. Her words bounced off him as though he wore a bulletproof vest.

Jules looked down at the crumpled ball of paper on her lap. Reading the contents of the report made her sick to her stomach. She had to get away from her office. Her sanctuary was the pediatric ward, where she could check on her young patients. If she could make them feel better, if only for a short while, maybe she could do the same for herself.

She knew that John Sinclair was a misogynist. He put every female nurse and doctor in pediatrics on edge with his sexist barbs and un-wanted advances. Jules stood up to him, at least she tried when he attempted to coax her into going out with him. His flattery seemed too sugary to be sincere. That night, when she tried to escape Sinclair's advances, something deep inside her told her that she had to put an end to it. She needed a hero to come to her rescue.

She gazed at Dane. What a hero he turned out to be. To think that she defended Sinclair to Bates made her feel ashamed. The report listed the names of several staff members who had filed sexual harassment complaints against John Sinclair while Jules worked in Toronto. It stated that John Sinclair was awaiting a hearing before the medical board.

Dane squeezed her hand. "Hey." His voice was low and rough.

Jules got to her feet and leaned over him. "Hey, yourself. How are you feeling?"

"Thirty years younger."

"What do you mean?"

"You have elf ears on your head and Santa on your stethoscope, and I think that's a reindeer peering out of your pocket. What happened? Did you move me to the pediatric ward so you could be my doctor?"

Jules' hand went to her head. She'd forgotten the headband she had put on when she made her rounds. Her cheeks burned, once again giving away her embarrassment.

"Don't be embarrassed, Red, I think they look kinda sexy." Dane winked at her as he smiled.

"We don't have a bed large enough for you in pediatrics."

"That's okay. I can squeeze into small spaces. I've had plenty of practice." He saw the sparkle leave her eyes and knew that she was thinking of what he did from those small spaces. "Don't go there, Red. Stay here. With me."

"I'm trying." She felt a sadness overcome her, one that she hadn't felt since her parents died. "I thought I could do this. I don't want to think about what you did, but it's too damned hard. It takes a word, one stupid word, and I'm reliving my parents' murder all over again. It's hard not to imagine you—"

"Don't. If being with me makes you sad, don't do it to yourself."

"It's not you. It's me!"

Dane gave a humorless laugh. "I've heard that one before. Don't worry, Red, I understand. You've got your moral high ground, and I've got my pride. I won't beg you to try to like me. Just promise me one thing."

"What is it?"

"Let me be a part of Becca's life. You don't have to tell her I'm her daddy. Just let me get to know her."

Jules wiped a tear from her eye. Damn him for being so understanding. "I promise."

"Good. Then get the hell out of my room, so I don't have to see the pity in your eyes."

He watched her leave, closing the door behind her and then felt the tremendous ache in his chest. He'd only felt that ache once before when his grandmother passed away. He had joked that he loved her twice as much as he would any woman because she was both his mother and his grandmother. It wasn't a joke. Dane felt her loss doubly hard, and he knew that losing Red would stay with him for the rest of his life.

Jules made her way to the hospital's daycare. She needed to see Becca and hold her in her arms.

"What's wrong, Mommy?" Becca asked when she met her at the daycare entrance. "You're crying."

Jules crouched and took Becca in her arms. "Mommy missed you and needed a hug. That's all, sweetheart."

"Do you want to hug Flopsy? He makes me feel better when I'm sad." Becca handed the stuffed rabbit to Jules so that she could put on her coat.

"When are you sad?" Jules asked while she helped Becca with her coat buttons.

"When I think about my daddy."

Jules stopped. "Your daddy?"

Becca nodded her head.

"Why does thinking about him make you sad?"

"He must be lonely. He doesn't have me, you, or Flopsy to make him feel better when he gets sad."

"What makes you think he gets sad?"

Becca gave Jules a knowing look, as though Jules should have known the answer without asking. "Because he doesn't have us, Mommy."

Jules took Becca into her arms and hugged her tight. "Oh, Becca. You have such a big heart. Mommy is so proud of you!"

"I have little ears, too, Mommy."

Chapter Twelve

"You should be staying home and resting."

Dane stood in front of the foyer mirror attempting to tie his bow tie. He could see Bates standing behind him, arms crossed across his chest and a frown on his face. He appreciated Bates' concern although he was getting tired of the nonstop mothering.

"I'm fine. Doc gave me the all-clear."

"You should have asked for a second opinion. Doc lets you get away with too much."

"Hers was the second opinion." Dane finished the tie and admired his accomplishment.

"You're crooked. Turn around and let me fix it."

"What would I do without you?"

"I'd hate to think," he grumbled. Bates stepped back and admired his work. "There. You look presentable now."

"Thank you."

Bates reached into his coat pocket and pulled out a wrapped present. "This is for the dog. For tonight. From Val."

Dane looked down at Lucky. "She buys you presents. It looks like I'm still in the doghouse." Dane unwrapped the present to find a dog collar with a black bow tie attached to it. He examined the intricate handwork. "She made this?"

Bates answered with a shrug.

"We'll have to remember to thank Auntie Val when we see her tomorrow."

"Since when did she become your Auntie Val?"

"She's not mine. She's Lucky's. At least that's how Becca sees it. It's kind of cute." Dane crouched beside his dog and placed the new collar around his neck. "What do you think, boy? You're going to be the beau of the ball." He adjusted Lucky's service vest. "I think we're ready. How about you, Uncle Bates?"

"I'm no one's Uncle Bates, especially his. He tried to take my arm off."

"He apologized with an expensive bottle of Canadian whiskey." Dane rubbed Lucky's head. "What more can he do to say he's sorry?"

Bates grunted.

"Come on, cheer up! You've got the night to yourself. Don't you have plans with a certain someone?"

"What's got you in such a good mood?"

"I'm always like this." Bates' knowing glance made him explain. "Jules is going to be there. I know she's dating someone else. It's Christmas. Maybe, just maybe, she might let me have one dance. That's all I want. Just one dance."

"Look, Boss, about the mission. I can look after it. You should concentrate on yourself and getting better."

Dane shook his head. "This mission is all that keeps me going. I have a daughter who doesn't know that I'm her father. Her mother sees me as a cold-blooded killer. Besides, she has someone else in her life. And before you say that can be changed, you know I don't take what's not mine. Jules has Blackwell. No more discussion. Do you hear me, Corporal?"

"Yes, Sir!"

They drove in silence to the gala. Dane's thoughts were on Jules. As much as he tried to keep her out, the temperamental redhead kept finding her way into his head. It wasn't her fault, not this time. He had learned through Val that Blackwell had invited Jules to the High River General Hospital's Christmas Gala. It was the hospital's biggest fundraiser, known for its grandeur and reputation as the best Christmas tradition in town.

Jules asked Val if she could look after Becca for the day while Jules spent the day at the salon getting pampered for the gala. From the intel Val could gather, Jules wanted to look her best tonight, hopeful that something memorable was going to happen. Jules was happy and excited. Val hadn't seen Jules like this in a very long time. Val didn't have to say more. Dane felt it in the pit of his stomach that tonight was the night. It was Christmas and what better time to get engaged than now. Blackwell was going to propose to Jules, and Jules was ready to accept. New Year's and Valentine's Day were clichés for getting engaged. But Christmas? If Dane had the chance, he would pick Christmas, his favorite time of the year.

"Call me when you're ready to go home."

Dane looked out the passenger window, realizing that they had arrived and Bates had stopped the SUV.

"Yes, Bates. I promise." He smiled at his friend. "Try to enjoy yourself. You deserve a fun night out."

Dane exited the SUV with Lucky. He closed his door and turned to face the entrance to the hotel. Taking in a deep breath, he squared his shoulders and prepared himself for what awaited him. Tonight was the night that the hospital's doctors and board members rubbed shoulders with the local philanthropists, thanking them for their current year's donations while hoping to get a commitment for funding High River General in the new year. Dane had already made this year's donation—a sizable amount toward the pediatric ward's latest project.

He hadn't attended a function as grand as this since his accident. It would be a good test for him and Lucky, dealing with the stares, the comments, and ignorance. It was all worth it if Jules would give him one dance.

Dane entered the hotel lobby and was immediately impressed by the Christmas decorations and their festive elegance. He gazed up at the eighteen-foot high Christmas tree decorated in shiny gold and silver hues. It was magnificent, although Dane thought it a bit much for his tastes. Old fashioned country was more his style with popcorn strands draped on the branches, and handmade family decorations passed down from generation to generation hung on the branches. He was sentimental that way with memories of family traditions shared with his grandparents. It seemed like a lifetime ago.

During his fourth tour, he spent Christmas in Afghanistan. Dane found himself dreaming of his favorite time of the year. He didn't have anyone special waiting for him, but if he did, he knew how he would make the Christmas holidays memorable for both of them. At night he'd take his special someone out to his ranch, have the sleigh readied and then take her on a sleigh ride across the fields. They would snuggle under a fur lap throw and drink his favorite blend of hot cocoa and Bailey's Irish Cream. Sleigh bells would jingle and the sound of the horses moving through the snow would be the only things they heard. They wouldn't talk, both of them taking in the moment. And then, when the time was right, and they stopped to gaze up at the moon and stars, Dane would take the ring box out of his pocket and ask her to marry him. She would gaze into his eyes, tears forming, and then she'd say—

"Andrews! Over here!"

Dane looked for the owner of the voice. He nodded, recognizing Hank Marshall, chairman of the hospital's board. Dane made his way toward the man and his wife, who stood in line to check their coats.

"Glad you made it. I wasn't sure if you'd accept our invitation," the portly gentleman said, offering his hand to Dane. "This is my wife, Mary."

Dane shook his hand. "It was your invitation that convinced me to come," Dane said, smiling. "He's a very persuasive man, your husband." Dane offered as he shook Mary's hand.

"It's nice to meet you. That's quite the dog you have. He looks so fierce. Are you sure it's safe to have him here?"

"Mary," her husband chuckled, his face reddening. "Don't be ridiculous. My apologies, Dane. My wife isn't a fan of dogs."

Lucky sat at Dane's feet.

"That's quite all right. His name is Lucky, and he's perfectly safe to be around as long as he's left alone to do his job. He doesn't like to be bothered when he's working."

Dane handed in his coat, dropping a ten dollar bill into the tip jar. Pocketing his coat check stub into his pants, he excused himself from the couple and made his way into the ballroom. Immediately greeted by a server, Dane took the offered glass of champagne from the silver tray. While sipping from his drink, he got his bearings—nine o'clock, twelve o'clock and three o'clock—exits, bars, seating area, stage, people. It was a habit of his, never forgotten. He always knew where he was, the layout of the room, how to enter, and how to escape. He didn't notice anyone of particular interest to him, only the familiar faces of the hospital's board of directors.

He saw the side glances and the whispers as he and Lucky made their way through the guests. "Looks like all eyes are on you, boy. I told you you'd be the beau of the ball."

She saw him first. There was no mistaking the reaction to Dane's arrival was for anyone but him. It was as though everyone in attendance stopped talking and turned their attention to watch him make his entrance into the room. For the last week, the gossip flowing through the hospital halls was of the mysterious benefactor who had made a sizeable donation to the pediatric ward. And so they guessed that the tall man in the designer tuxedo with a large dog at his side had to be the mysterious donor.

Dane looked handsome and dressed to kill, as though he had stepped off a GQ magazine cover or a women's magazine with the heading *Dream Date*. Jules smiled at the comparison she made, realizing that the man making his way through the room was no fantasy. He was real. Her heart skipped a beat when he caught her watching him from across the room. A wink was all it took to bring a blush to her face.

"Here he comes," Mark whispered in her ear.

"I see him." Jules sipped nervously from her champagne glass.

"Are you okay?"

"I'm fine."

"Take a deep breath, Jules."

"Stop it, Mark. Please."

She felt his hand on her hip. Jules turned her head to look at Mark. "What are you doing?"

"You're shaking. Can't have you falling at the man's feet, can I?"

Jules shook her head. "You think I'm foolish, don't you?"

"For you? Yes. You're not the Jules Montgomery I know when you're around him. You can't mention his name without—"

"Dane, you're here!" Jules gushed, interrupting Mark.

"I'm not late, am I?" Dane asked as he held out his hand to Mark. "Good to see you again, Blackwell."

"Same here."

"Jules, you look exquisite." Dane held his hand out to her. His gaze took in every inch of her. She wore a deep green velvet ball gown with a V-neck that complemented her breasts. The A-line symmetry flowed from her waist accentuated with sparkling gemstones. And her hair, she wore it long, cascading waves falling past her shoulders. "You're wearing my favorite colors."

She took his hand and held on to it. "Thank you for letting Val stay with Becca. They've had a wonderful day together."

"No need to thank me. Val is free to do as she pleases. She's been sending me pictures of the two of them all day. She adores Becca, as we all do."

"How are you feeling?"

Dane pulled his gaze away from Jules. It was torture to do so to answer Blackwell. "I'm well. Thanks for asking. I hear I gave everyone a scare. Val is still reminding me of it."

"You gave all of us a scare."

Dane returned his gaze to Jules. "I'm told there's a seating plan. Do you happen to know where I'm supposed to go?"

"You're with us."

Dane nodded his agreement.

"We're at the front. The organizers thought it best to keep your dog out of everyone's way."

"Mark! You don't have to say it like that!"

"It's okay, Jules. I appreciate the consideration. Lucky is rather big to have to step around. After you." Dane gestured for Jules and Mark to lead him to their table.

Something was off. Mark walked without touching Jules. He should have offered his arm for her to hold or his hand. And if not that, the palm of his hand should be on her hip or lower back to guide her. Not that Dane wanted to see another man's hands on Red, but if anyone should be touching her, it should be Mark.

They took their seats with Jules sitting between the two men. Lucky lay down between Jules' and Dane's chairs.

"Is that enough room for him?"

"Don't worry. Lucky will make it work."

"Does he get something to eat when we're eating?"

"He's working, Jules. He eats at breakfast."

Dane and Mark both stood when the rest of their table arrived. They exchanged pleasantries with Hank and Mary Marshall, along with two other members of the board and their spouses.

"Tell me honestly, are red and green your favorite colors?"

"I never lie. I've loved the colors since I was a child. You wearing green tonight only reinforces why they still are."

"Always the charmer."

Dane chuckled. "Is that what you think I'm doing?"

"You have a way of saying the right thing. If I remember correctly, the night we met, you said all the right things."

"They were all true."

"Excuse me. I hope you don't mind me asking, but what is wrong with you that you need a service dog?"

An awkward silence surrounded the table. And in that instant, Dane diffused it, giving the older woman who asked the question a warm smile.

"I have a brain injury. My dog can smell a seizure about to happen and alerts me so that I can make myself safe. Without Lucky, I wouldn't have this handsome face you've been admiring."

The woman responded with a smile.

"He can smell it?" her husband asked.

"A dog's nose has up to three hundred million sensory receptors in its nose, whereas we only have about six million. Lucky's nose can detect so much more than ours, and he can remember various scents. Before I have a seizure, my body chemistry changes. I don't feel anything, and yet Lucky smells it right away. He can detect it within five minutes. Some dogs can sense seizures before that. I won't complain. I can react quickly and make myself safe within five minutes."

"Fascinating."

"Amazing."

Jules leaned into Dane and whispered in his ear, "Charming."

While they enjoyed their meal and the free-flowing wine, the table fell into easy conversation mostly centered around Dane. He answered their questions in a relaxed manner and tried his best to turn the subject away from him, but failed.

"Tell them about your stint as a firefighter," Jules teased.

"You were a firefighter?"

"No, Jules has me confused with someone else."

"The two of you know each other?"

They turned and looked at each other, giving each other a knowing smile.

"We met on a blind date a few years ago."

"Unfortunately, it was right before Jules left for Toronto, so we didn't have the chance to get to know each other."

"What about now?"

"Jules has someone in her life. I'm too late." Dane got to his feet. "If you'll excuse me, Lucky needs a bathroom break."

"I'll go with you," Jules offered as she got to her feet.

"No. Stay here with Mark. I won't take long. Let's go, boy."

Jules watched as Dane left the ballroom.

Mark reached for her hand. "Jules, sit down. He'll be back."

She sat down reluctantly. "This isn't going as I planned."

"Plans rarely do. Don't roll your eyes at me. You know it's true."

"It doesn't mean I like to hear you say it."

"Talk to him. Once the dinner finishes and the speeches end, you'll have the chance."

"What if he doesn't want to talk?"

"Then make him listen. You can do that."

Dane pulled the collar of his tuxedo jacket up against his neck to block the cold without little effect. It was cold as hell outside, typical for Alberta.

"Hurry up, boy. Do your business."

He waited while Lucky sniffed various poles and bushes to piss on. Dane always marveled at how well controlled a dog's bladder was— that a dog could piss in tiny amounts stop and then go again stop and then go again. A dog's bladder never seemed to be empty. Unless he'd been sleeping all night and that morning piss was the longest and most satisfying of the day. If Lucky could talk, Dane knew that he'd agree with him on that point.

"Let's go."

Dane gave a light tug on Lucky's leash. As he turned to make his way back to the hotel entrance, he glimpsed a shadow, a face hidden among potted trees and shrubs. Dane stood still for a moment trying to find the form again. It was gone.

"You had me worried," Jules whispered when he rejoined their table.

"Why? I told you I'd be back."

His eyes had changed, becoming darker, dangerous looking.

"What's wrong?"

"Nothing."

"No lies, remember?"

"I'm not lying. There's nothing wrong." He winked at her as though a wink would magically put her at ease. "When does the dancing start? It would be nice to have one dance with you before the clock strikes midnight."

"Hold your horses, Prince Charming. Don't you have a speech to give first?"

"I can say I'm not feeling well. Coming down with a seizure or something."

"Don't joke about something like that!" Jules put her hand on his arm. "Are you joking, or do you feel unwell?"

"I'm fine." Dane surveyed the room, feeling unease, knowing that someone was watching them. He was sure of it. The only question was, who? It wouldn't be Bates. Bates had watched him before without giving him this feeling. No. This time it was someone else.

A man's voice crackled over the speaker, "May I have your attention, please?"

Dane turned his gaze to the stage where the Director of Fundraising was fidgeting with the microphone.

"On behalf of the High River General Hospital Fundraising Committee, I would like to welcome all of you to our Christmas Gala. It is our way of thanking you, our generous supporters, for your generosity toward our fine hospital." He paused for applause. "It is my pleasure to introduce you to Mr. Dane Andrews, who has pledged ongoing support for a new project for our pediatric wing. Please give a warm welcome to Mr. Dane Andrews."

Dane got to his feet. Immediately Lucky was standing before him, waiting for a command. Dane unleashed him before making his way to the stage. It was an impressive sight, the way Lucky stuck to Dane's side, never wavering or leaving an inch between them. They were man and dog inseparable, giving no notice of the applause that filled the room.

He didn't want to have his biography read aloud to the audience. His past was of no concern to them, nothing that he wanted them to know, especially his role in the Special Elite. Retired Naval Master Corporal was all they needed to know. Dane shook the director's hand then took the offered microphone. He didn't stand behind the lectern, allowing everyone to get the full view of Lucky who stood beside him, watching his every move.

"Thank you. I am honored to speak to you tonight. You may have noticed that I have a dog with me. His name is Lucky, and he is my service dog. He's wearing a bow tie because his aunt thought he should look his best for tonight. He wears this red vest to alert people that he is working and that he shouldn't be disturbed. You can tell that he's working because he isn't leaving my side." Dane took a few steps to his left and then to his right as if they were dancing. Lucky moved with him. "When we're out in public, this is what he does. I won't go into great detail, only to tell you that I have seizures and it's Lucky's job to let me know when I am about to have one and then to keep me safe while I have it. It's because of Lucky and the freedom he has given me to lead a relatively normal life, that I met with the Board of Directors and discussed with them the possibility of providing service dogs to children in need.

"Service dogs can give children the confidence and freedom to be themselves. And they can provide parents peace of mind knowing that their child is safe. There are so many types of service dogs. I can't list them all, but here are a few services they can provide: they can help the visually impaired, the autistic, the physically disabled, and those who have epilepsy. Dogs are intelligent and intuitive. Whatever their training, service dogs help adults and children lead independent lives. It is my pledge, and I hope you make it yours as well, to support our service dog project."

Dane looked behind him and nodded to the band. He turned to face the audience, "It looks like the band is ready to play, and I know that I'd like to get in a dance or two. So please, consider supporting this very worthwhile cause. Thank you."

Dane handed the microphone to a stagehand standing by the stairs as he made his exit. Applause followed him to his table. Jules and Mark were the first to rise to greet him.

"What a wonderful idea, Dane. I had no idea," Mark said as he shook his hand.

"I hope one of those dances is with me," Jules said to him.

"Of course. I wouldn't want to dance with anyone else."

The band started to play.

"May I have this dance?" Dane asked. "That is if Mark doesn't want the first dance with you."

"Go ahead, Andrews. She's all yours."

"What about Lucky?"

Dane glanced at his dog. "Sit this one out okay, boy? Stay."

Dane placed the palm of his hand on the small of Jules' back and escorted her to the dance floor.

"He'll stay?"

"If he senses anything, he'll come and get me."

"You're sure?"

Dane held Jules in his arms and started to dance. "His nose can find me anywhere in this room. I'm sure he'll let me know if he senses anything. And if he doesn't, at least I'll be surrounded by doctors if I do seize."

"I worry about you."

Dane smiled. "Thanks, but there's no need."

"Val's worried about you, too. There has to be a reason for what happened to you last week. Are you sure—"

"Let's drop it okay, Red? I don't want to waste what could be my only dance with the most beautiful woman in the room talking about my brain."

"Most beautiful?"

"Always." Dane kissed her forehead. "I thought so when I first met you, and I still do."

"Dane—"

"Mark's a lucky guy. I think the two of you make a great couple. He seems to like Becca, too. That's important."

"Why are you talking like that? Do you know something I don't?"

"Red, it's Christmas. You look like a million dollars in that dress. You're with a man who adores you. It's obvious to me that tonight is a special night for the two of you. It's the perfect time to get engaged. You have my approval."

Jules laughed. "I have your approval? That's sweet, although unnecessary."

"Why?"

"Mark and I aren't getting engaged. We aren't even dating. I don't know how you got that idea. Did Val say something?"

"No one said anything. I just assumed."

"You know what they say about people who assume, Gary." There it was, the smile that he had missed and the sparkle in her eyes. "Mark's gay. His partner is out of town. He invited me to join him tonight. That's all."

Dane stopped, both of them stood in the middle of the dance floor, staring at each other. It was now Dane's turn to show his embarrassment, although he didn't turn red. He had that deer caught in the headlights look—stunned.

"So if you didn't dress like this for Mark, who did you dress for?"

"Can't a woman dress up for herself?"

"Of course she can. It's just that—"

"It's just what, Gary?" Jules moved in closer to him, pressing her body against his.

"You hate me."

"I don't hate you. I've never said that."

Dane looked into her eyes. There was no sign of deceit, but he knew what she thought about him. He had seen the pity she felt for him, and the sadness that he made her feel. "The last time we spoke, you made it clear that you couldn't be with me without being reminded of your parents' murders. You hate what I do. You hate guns and guns are a part of my life. I can't change that."

"I'm not asking you to change that or anything else."

"Don't play games with me. Not now."

"This isn't a game. I promise."

"Then tell me why the sudden change of heart. I haven't done anything. I haven't changed."

"That's where you're wrong. We have a beautiful daughter who has the biggest heart of anyone I know. As much as I'd like to take credit for giving her that heart, I know that she gets it from you."

"That still doesn't explain why."

"It's Becca. She's made me see things differently. I have to let go of the sadness. I can't let my parents' deaths keep me from being happy. I can hate guns, but I don't have to keep you out of my life because of them. We deserve to be happy, Dane. We deserve to be happy together."

Dane forced himself to look away. He had to think. Jules had caught him off guard, saying things he never expected to hear. All Dane hoped for was a dance. And now she was telling him that she wanted to be happy with him. Dane straightened. There it was again, a man's face in the shadows watching him. When the man realized that Dane had spotted him, he made his way to an exit and escaped.

"What is it?" Jules asked.

He shook his head. "Nothing."

"Dane, people are staring at us. Are we going to dance?"

Before he could answer, Lucky bumped his hand with his wet nose.

"No, this can't be happening." Dane looked down at his dog. "Your timing sucks, boy."

"Dane, what is it?"

"I'm about to go down. I need to find a place to crash."

"Come with me." Jules took Dane by the hand and led him out of the ballroom. Lucky stayed by Dane's side.

Dane nodded toward the lobby. "There's a quiet spot around the corner. I noticed it when I came in." Jules pulled on his arm, quickening her pace. "We don't have to run, Red. I've got time."

"Humor me. I don't know how you do this."

Dane chuckled. "Neither do I. There," he said when he spotted a quiet nook with a bench long enough to accommodate his body. Perfect for quiet talks or hushed phone calls. "This will do."

Dane took off his tuxedo jacket and folded it to make a pillow for his head before he laid out on the bench. Immediately Lucky jumped onto his chest. Dane's hand rested on Lucky's back.

"Why does he do that?"

"His weight comforts me, especially when I come out of it."

"What can I do for you?"

"Don't let anyone try to rob me."

"Dane—"

"Tell me why you want to be happy with me."

He was gone before Jules could say the words. It was strange to sit with him while he had his seizure. Dane laid perfectly still as though he were asleep. Lucky rested his head on Dane's shoulder.

Jules took hold of Dane's hand and held it. "Look after him, boy. Keep him safe."

She sat in silence, listening to Dane as he breathed, afraid that maybe it would stop. Jules thought back to when she was a new mom, alone in her home with her newborn baby. She would sit by Becca's crib for hours listening to her breathe, afraid that the breathing might stop. Jules was a doctor. She knew the odds and yet she still worried. And then she thought of him, her fantasy man who gave her this remarkable baby and she wondered who he was, and she wished he was with her.

Lucky whined, wagging his tail while licking Dane's face. Dane's hand moved on his dog's back, giving him slow caresses.

"Dane?" Jules waited for him to respond. She squeezed his hand.

"Mmm." He kept his eyes closed.

"I'm here for you."

"No one tried to rob me?"

"No."

"What were we talking about before I blacked out?"

"I don't remember."

"Liar." A thin smile formed on his face.

"Are you going to open your eyes?"

"No, then I can pretend this is a dream if you don't tell me why you want us to be happy together."

"Because of Becca."

"Becca?"

"Her heart. Remember? She got it from you."

"It's only DNA." His voice was soft, but the words stung, a painful reminder of what she had said to him.

"I'm sorry that I said that to you. You're more than a DNA donor."

"Careful, Red, you might get my hopes up."

She sighed heavily. "Will you open your eyes? I feel as though I'm talking to a corpse."

One eye opened. "Played that game before, doc?"

"I can make it happen if you want," she said with a low, threatening tone.

Dane's other eye opened. "I'm listening."

"Becca needs to have you in her life as her father. And I need to have you in my life, too."

"As?"

"As my boyfriend."

"Boyfriend?"

"Let's not rush things. I want to do this right this time around. No shortcuts. Let's start at the beginning and see where we go from there."

"Okay." Dane's eyes closed.

"Dane?"

"Give me a minute." They stayed for a quiet moment, not moving. Lucky on top of Dane, waiting for his command. Jules kept hold of Dane's hand and waited for one word that would tell her he was back. A simple word that meant so much in its uttering.

"Off."

Lucky jumped off Dane, immediately sitting by the bench, his attention focused on his master.

"Jules?"

"I'm here."

"I love you."

Chapter Thirteen

"Won't Bates mind?"

"He'll be relieved not to have to come pick me up. He won't know what to do with his freedom."

"He didn't sound happy from what I could hear."

"He never sounds happy."

"I can't argue with that."

Dane pulled Jules into his side as they took a taxi to her townhouse. Jules gave quick goodbyes to Mark and their tablemates while Dane waited in the lobby. His seizure had nearly exhausted him, and he wanted to spend the last of his energy in the company of his Red.

She snuggled into the warmth of his coat. "How much longer?"

"We're almost there."

"Val will be happy to see you all dressed up."

"You think so?"

"Every time we talk, she has to mention your name and how wonderful you are. She throws Becca's name in, too, for good measure. As though I needed to be convinced to fall for you."

"Didn't you?"

She didn't answer him right away. Instead, she played with a button on his coat.

"Ignoring the question doesn't make it go away, Red."

"I'm not ignoring it. It's just that if I say the words, it will make me think of the time wasted."

"Time hasn't been wasted. Everything happens the way it should."

"The eternal optimist."

"You could say that. And the other thing that you haven't said yet."

Jules swatted at him playfully. "You don't let things go."

"Not when I want an answer."

Jules breathed in deeply, letting the air out slowly. "You win. I love you, too, although we're not going to rush things. I want to do this romance thing right."

"Romance thing? Didn't we do it right the night we met? How much practice do we need?"

"This time you're Dane, and I'm Jules. This time we'll learn everything about each other without making up stories. This time—"

"It will be for keeps." Dane kissed the top of Jules' head. "Do you think Val will be up? Because once I get you into your house, I'd like some private time with you."

The taxi pulled into Jules' driveway and stopped. Dane paid the driver then exited the cab with Lucky. Jules waited for Dane to open her door, somehow knowing that he would want her to. Her door opened, and his hand reached in, offering her assistance.

"Careful, it's a bit slippery."

Jules linked her arm through Dane's as they made it slowly to her front door.

"Keys?"

"I can open my front door."

He gave her a sideways glance, letting her know that there were some things she shouldn't argue. Jules handed them to him. Dane slid the key into the lock and opened the door.

"Go on, boy," he ordered as he motioned with his head.

Lucky stepped in, and the hairs on the ridge on his back immediately stood on end while a low growl rumbled from his chest.

"Stay here." Dane's voice was low and commanding.

"What is it?" Jules whispered.

"I don't know. I'll take a look."

"Becca!" Jules grabbed onto Dane's arm.

"Shh. I've got this. If I'm not back in twenty seconds, call Bates. Tell him we may have an intruder."

"Dane—"

"Promise me you'll stay here. You won't come inside until I tell you to."

"I promise."

"Good. I've got this, Jules. Now start timing me."

Dane eased his way into the house, keeping Lucky on a short leash. He couldn't risk the dog charging at a stranger, especially one who could be armed. Dane needed to assess this situation, keep his cool, and not get anyone hurt or killed. Every light in the house seemed to be turned on, a clear give away that something was amiss. Val didn't like a dark house, but this was overkill even for her.

Lucky tugged at his leash, pulling Dane down the hallway toward the kitchen. Dane kept close to the wall, advancing in slow, measured steps.

"Val?"

He heard muffled sounds in response coming from ahead of him. Lucky whined, tugging harder at his leash.

"Easy, boy. Steady."

"Don't be scared, Dane, or do you prefer the name Gary?"

He knew that voice. Dane made his way to the kitchen entrance and stopped. He took in the situation, instantly seeing broken glass in the kitchen door, Val seated on a stool, her mouth gagged and her hands tied behind her back. John Sinclair stood at her side with a pistol pointed at her head. Dane recognized the type of gun, a Walther PPK, small and accurate.

Lucky barked, pulling at his leash to get to the intruder.

Sinclair aimed the pistol at him. "Shut him up, or else he's dead."

"Quiet."

Lucky obeyed. He sat at Dane's feet, whining.

Sinclair resumed pointing the gun at Val.

"Put the gun down, Sinclair. There's no need for it."

"Where is she? Where's Jules?"

"Outside." Dane saw the terror in Val's eyes. One cheek redder than the other, showing the start of a bruise. "You're going to be okay, Val."

"Bring Jules inside."

Dane shook his head. "You know I can't do that. Why are you here?"

"I'm righting a wrong. Five years ago, you cheated me, and now it's time for me to collect what you owe me."

Dane frowned. "What are you owed?"

"You and Jules played me for a fool. Tried to make me believe that you were involved, but you weren't. You lied."

"We were involved. It wasn't a lie."

"Don't give me that bullshit. Jules called you Gary and said that you were a bush firefighter. You're no more a firefighter than I am. I was at the gala tonight. I saw the two of you."

In an instant, Dane recognized the face in the shadows as being Sinclair's and wondered how he had missed it.

"Okay, so I'm not a firefighter, but Jules and I were involved. We were playing a game, one she didn't want to play with you. She wasn't interested in you then and she sure as hell isn't interested in you now."

"She would be if you weren't in the picture."

Dane laughed. "Never."

Sinclair pointed the gun at Dane. "Don't laugh at me!"

"I'm not laughing at you. It's Jules. Do you think you're the only one she's burned? She left me after that night. No note. No goodbye, just gone. She treated me the same way she did you. She's moved on, Sinclair. She's got someone else in her life who she's serious about big time. If you don't believe me, ask Val. Oh wait, you can't, she's gagged."

"Dane?" A child's voice called out to him from down the hallway.

"Who is there?" Sinclair asked, still holding the pistol to Val's head.

Dane turned his head slightly, enough so that he could see Becca with eyes wide open hugging Flopsy to her chest. She stood outside of Jules' office door.

"Becca, remember your secret hiding spot? Go there now. Hide, Becca. Hide."

Dane turned his attention back to Sinclair. "Touch one hair on that child's head, and you die."

John Sinclair laughed. "Now who's laughing? I have the gun, Andrews. You have nothing."

"You're wrong. I have everything."

Jules promised Dane she wouldn't enter the house. It was the hardest promise she had ever made in her life, and the longest twenty seconds she could remember. When Jules called Bates, begging him to help Dane, he made her promise, too. She waited on the doorstep, shivering in the cold winter air and cried.

Within minutes, Bates arrived in front of her house. He left the SUV with the engine running and made his way to Jules.

"Any change?"

She shook her head.

"Get in the car and stay there. It's the safest place for you to be. Go!"

Jules looked back at the house. Every maternal fiber in her being called out to her to rush into that house and save her child.

"I've got this. Now go!"

Jules slid down the driveway, struggling to keep from falling. She reached the vehicle and pulled at the door, scrambled inside, then closed the door. Jules stared out of the window, praying for her child and Val, and the two men rescuing them.

Bates reached into his coat pocket and pulled out his pistol before opening the front door quietly. From the foyer, he could see Dane's back to him with one hand behind his back, signaling him—one shooter, standing. Dane laughed. A dead give away that he was stalling for time until reinforcements arrived. He always kept his cool. Dane trained for it, but his demeanor went far beyond training. While on tour facing the deadliest of battles, Bates often wondered how his partner kept his shit together when everyone around him lost it. It wasn't optimism. It wasn't faith. It was something Bates had yet to figure out.

Bates cleared his head, focusing on the task at hand. Making his way through the living room to the kitchen, he stayed alert, listening to the conversation. Dane dropped clues, letting Bates know the situation. Val was alive and gagged. By the angle of Dane's stance, Bates knew the position of the intruder. His back would be to Bates. If only Dane could keep the bastard occupied, Bates would have a clear shot.

"What do you mean that you have everything?"

Dane shifted on his feet, trying to draw Sinclair away from Val.

"I have more than I want, Sinclair. Quite frankly, I could do without some of it. I'd be happy to share it with you if you'd like."

"What are you talking about?"

"Cancer. I've got a tumor growing right here." Dane pointed to the top of his head. As he did so, he couldn't help but notice Val's eyes open wide, and tears start to form. "It was a helluva shock. Especially now, when I thought I was getting my life back."

"I'm not falling for your lies."

"I don't lie, Sinclair. I'm a man of my word. If a man can't stand by his word, he's nothing."

"It shouldn't matter then if I shoot you. You're going to die anyway." Sinclair aimed his pistol at Dane.

"Except for one thing. I don't plan to die."

At that moment, a shot rang out. John Sinclair crumpled to the floor as Dane lunged for Val. He grabbed her and pulled her off the stool and away from Sinclair's fallen form.

Bates entered the room, kicking away Sinclair's weapon before he kneeled beside him. He rolled him to his back.

"I should have killed you when I first saw you, you son of a bitch." Confirming that his target wasn't seriously injured, he added, "Looks like you're going to live."

Dane untied Val's gag and hands. "You're okay?"

"You have cancer?"

"Just a bit." Dane glanced over at Bates. "Jules?"

"She's in the car waiting. What about Becca?"

"Shit!"

Dane ran to Jules' office. He made his way to the desk and found Lucky underneath it, on guard. Lucky's backside pressed against the secret hiding spot as he looked out from under the desk. The hairs on his back stood at attention, threatening anyone who dared come near him.

"Good boy. Let's get her out."

Lucky barked once as though he were telling Dane to hurry up. He turned his body to face the underside of the desk with his nose pressed to the wooden panel.

Dane reached under the desk, feeling for the disk that would release Becca from her hiding place. It would have been easier without Lucky's nose in the way, but Dane thought it best if the first friendly face Becca saw was Lucky's. Pressing the disk, Dane waited for the drawer to open.

"Lucky! You found me!"

Dane smiled at the sound of the sweetest voice he had ever heard.

Lucky whined his excitement, and his wagging tail thumped against the desk. His licks to Becca's face brought about cherubic giggling.

"Becca!" Jules called out to her from behind Dane.

"She's fine, Jules. Come on out, Becca. Mommy wants to see you."

Dane got to his feet. "Lucky, come, boy."

Lucky crawled out from under the desk with the little girl by his side.

Jules bent down, scooping her daughter into her arms and hugged her tight.

"She didn't see anything," Dane said softly.

"Mommy, I hid again, and Lucky found me. I like this game."

It had been a long night. Dealing with the emergency medical services and then giving statements to the police took its toll on everyone. Dane made the assurance that further questions would be answered the next day once a good night's sleep provided clearer heads. The house, now a crime scene, had to be vacated. Dane brought his family to his home. Their home.

"When were you going to tell me?" Jules had changed into a tank top and pajama bottoms.

"After Christmas." Dane handed Jules her drink. "I didn't want to ruin the holidays." He wore a T-shirt with boxer shorts since he had never been a fan of pajamas.

"Val is pissed at you."

Dane took a long swallow of his Scotch. "She can yell at me tomorrow if she wants to. You can, too if you want. Right now, I want us to sleep."

He placed his glass on his bedside table before falling onto his bed.

"It is tomorrow."

"Later tomorrow then."

"She really should be in bed." Jules gazed at her sleeping daughter cuddled up to Lucky on his overly large dog bed with a blanket over them.

"She's fine. Besides, you didn't want to leave her alone, and I want you here with me."

"She's sleeping on the floor."

"I've slept in worse places. Trust me. Becca's fine."

Jules placed her unfinished drink beside Dane's glass. "I trust you. More than anyone else in the world, I trust you." She gazed down at him. Tears welled in her eyes.

"There's a but coming."

"I've never been so scared in my life. When you went into the house not knowing what you'd find. And I was left outside to think the worst. Becca and Val—"

Dane opened his arms to her. "I wouldn't let anything happen to them."

Jules lowered herself onto him, snuggling into the warm hardness of his chest. Dane held her tight as his hands caressed her back in a soothing motion.

"I love you with all my heart."

"I know what you mean. I love you, too."

They lay in silence for a long moment.

"You'll always be my Gary."

"Always."

Chapter Fourteen

DANE AWOKE to soft kisses and heavy pressure on his chest. His left hand reached for the owner of the mouth that had the worst case of morning breath he had ever known. Lucky. Dane smiled and rubbed the head of his beloved dog. "Good morning to you, too," he said quietly.

His right arm felt heavy. Another weight kept it pinned to the mattress. Dane turned his head to find two redheads asleep beside him. Becca had wormed her way in between Jules and Dane, and Jules was the one making use of Dane's arm for a pillow. He smiled, realizing that the warm and fuzzy feeling he was experiencing was what the men in his unit described when they talked about being at home with their families. There was nothing like this—peace and contentment that Dane had never known. The feeling of family. His family.

Lucky nudged Dane.

"I know, boy. Time for a pee. Me, too. Off."

Lucky jumped to the floor and waited for Dane.

Special Elite training didn't prepare Dane for the moves necessary for extricating himself from a little girl and her mother without waking them. Becca rolled into the space he once occupied. Jules muttered something in her sleep before snuggling into her pillow.

Trying his best to be quiet, Dane slipped into stealth mode, not making a sound while making his way to his bathroom. Lucky followed, stopping in the doorway to give his master some semblance of privacy. Dane knew it was silly. He couldn't urinate if Lucky stood beside him watching. It was a guy thing. Guys didn't look at other guys pissing.

When he went to wash his hands and brush his teeth, seeing two toothbrushes, one small and the other regular, next to his in the glass, made him smile. *They're home, where they belong.*

The aroma of freshly brewed coffee and fresh out of the oven muffins greeted Dane as he entered the kitchen.

"Good morning," he said to Bates as he continued to walk to the back door.

Bates nodded.

"Go on, boy. Have your pee." Dane opened the door for his dog. He closed the door and watched Lucky through the glass. "Where's Val?"

"She'll be back," Bates answered as he moved from the table to refill his coffee mug.

"Back from where?"

"She's still pissed. Started crying, so she left to get her self together." He took an empty cup and filled it for Dane before returning to the table.

Dane opened the kitchen door. "Let's go. C'mon boy." Lucky came bounding into the kitchen then sat on the mat. "Good boy." Dane praised his dog as he took a towel and wiped the dog's snow-covered feet. "Time for breakfast."

Lucky waited patiently while Dane prepared his meal.

"That dog eats better than a lot of people in the world."

"It's a fair trade. He eats well so we can do our job saving the world even if it's one child at a time."

Dane gave Lucky his food then joined Bates at the harvest table.

"Thank you."

Bates nodded. "I should have killed the bastard."

Dane shook his head. "No. Val didn't need to see that. It's enough that we've seen our share of death in the world."

"When were you going to tell us?"

Both men turned their attention to the doorway leading to Val's private quarters.

Dane stood up and moved toward Val. "How are you? That's quite the bruise you have."

Val raised a hand to her face and touched the tender spot. "Does it look bad?"

"It makes you look badass. Doesn't it, Bates?"

"Yep."

"Last night, you were awesome. Special Elite awesome." Dane gave her a boyish wink.

"Stop it. I was no such thing." Tears welled in her eyes.

"Don't cry, Val." Dane took her in his arms. "Please don't cry."

"You can't die. Not now."

"I don't plan on dying. Not for quite some time. I've got lots to live for now that I have a family. Do you think I'd let anything happen to me?" Dane kissed the top of her head. "I've got a tumor. Doc says I've had it for a while, but it's only now that it's become visible. They're going to cut it out, and I'll be as good as new. If I'm lucky, my seizures will be gone, too."

"Why didn't you tell us?"

"It's Christmas. I was selfish. I didn't want to ruin it for anyone."

"Did Jules know?"

"I found out last night," Jules answered from across the room.

"Geez," Dane teased. "Do you ladies have to sneak up on us like that?"

Jules made her way to Dane. "Blame Bates. We've learned from the best."

"How's Becca?" Dane invited her into a group hug with Val.

"She's still sleeping."

"Good."

"Everything's going to work out. Don't worry about me. Okay?" He kissed Jules' forehead.

"Has anyone heard from the police? Have they charged John Sinclair?" Jules asked

"He's being taken care of," Bates answered.

"I'm making breakfast and no one better not say they're not hungry," Val announced as she pulled away from Dane and made her way to the kitchen counter.

"We're all hungry," Dane answered for them. They owed Val to eat a hearty breakfast, after what she had endured last night without a single complaint.

"I don't understand why he wanted Jules," Val mused.

"I was the only one who got away," Jules answered with deep sadness. "If only I'd dealt with him and not left for Toronto. Maybe he wouldn't have had the chance to hurt those other women."

"It's not your fault," Bates said. "He's been hurting women for a very long time."

"He's right," Dane agreed. "No one knows what would have happened if you had stayed."

"He's locked up now, and he won't be able to hurt anyone else," Bates said.

"Amen to that. Now someone set the table," Val said.

Chapter Fifteen

It was Christmas Eve night, two days since their ordeal with John Sinclair. Jules and Becca had not returned to their house in the city. As Jules explained to her aunt, she didn't want to waste any more time apart from Dane. Besides, Becca deserved the chance to get to know her father.

"Hurry up!" Dane called from the foyer. "We're melting here."

Becca jumped on the spot, unable to contain her excitement. "Come on, Mommy!"

"I'm coming," Jules answered, laughing. "Is all this necessary?" Jules appeared wearing an overly large tan sheepskin coat that hung to her knees, a thick buffalo wool knitted hat, and a red scarf around her neck. The only items belonging to her were her winter boots and whatever clothes she wore underneath the coat.

"Did you put on the long underwear?"

"No."

"Why not?"

"Because it's yours and it's too big. If I have to wear it to go outside, then I'm staying in the house. I already look ridiculous as it is. Look at me. I can barely move."

"You, Red, can never look ridiculous." Dane handed her a pair of sheepskin mittens. "You'll need these."

"Where are we going?" Jules asked as she put on the mitts.

"Out."

"Why do I have all these clothes on when you don't?" Jules noticed Dane wearing his sheepskin jacket and his Stetson. Becca wore her snowsuit, hat and mittens, and winter boots.

"I have my long underwear on, and I've got my scarf and gloves. I'm good."

Jules huffed in response, feeling uncomfortable and foolish in her winter wear.

"Where's Lucky? Shouldn't he be coming with us?"

"He's with Bates and Val." Dane held out his hand to her. "Don't worry. If anything happens to me, you can lie on top of me. You're pretty good at that."

Jules felt the blush rise in her cheeks. "That's not funny."

"It is, and it's true."

They left the warmth of the house into the frigid night air. Jules, too focused on trying to move in her heavy clothing, didn't notice the horse and sleigh waiting at the end of the walkway.

"Are you sure we shouldn't have Lucky?" Jules stopped when she noticed what was waiting in front of her. "Dane?"

Dane moved behind her, wrapping his arms around her waist. His mouth caressed her ear. "Care to help a guy out? Your name's Red and I'm Gary. You're my girlfriend. And this time we have a chaperone, Becca."

Underneath the scarf covering her mouth, Jules smiled. "What took you so long, Gary? A girl could freeze her ass off out here in the cold."

"That's my girl."

Dane took Jules by the hand and led her to the sleigh. "Step up and sit down and slide over."

She did as she was told, climbing up onto the sleigh then sitting on the cushioned seat.

"Slide over," Dane reminded her before he picked up Becca and handed her to Jules.

Dane followed behind her, taking his place on the padded seat. He reached behind him and retrieved a fur lap throw. "Put it on like this," he said as he positioned the wrap to cover their feet right up to their waists. "Are you ready?"

"Yes!"

Dane gathered the reins and gave them a shake. "Walk on, Beau."

"Are you sure this is safe?"

"I've been driving a sleigh since I was knee high to my grandfather."

"That's not what I meant."

"If I keel over, take the reins and tell Beau to go home. He'll turn around."

"You're joking."

"He's trained, just like Lucky. I wouldn't take the chance. If you can't do it, I'm sure Becca could."

"What are you? A dog and horse whisperer?"

Dane chuckled. "I'm a man who had too much time on his hands who wanted to get his life back as best he could."

"You've succeeded."

"Almost. Do you remember our first date after Marylou's wedding?"

And so it began—Gary and Red's make believe date.

"Perfectly. Do you?"

"How could I forget? It was February, close to Valentine's. We both agreed that Valentine's Day was pure hype and caused more heartbreak than any other day of the year."

"You still gave me a Valentine's card, though. It was a kid's card. No romance, only a cute kitten on the front. And you gave me a book."

"A book of fairy tales."

"Yes. You wrote on the first page. Something like—"

"Sometimes, life is more magical than a fairy tale. All you have to do is believe."

"You were right. Life is more magical than any fairy tale."

Dane handed the reins to Becca. "Want to give it a try?"

Becca squealed her delight.

"Hold them like this," Dane said, showing her how to hold the thick leather straps. "Got it?"

Becca nodded.

"That's my girl. You're doing great."

"Can she do that? Is she safe?"

"She's fine. Nothing's going to happen." Dane reached behind the seat and retrieved a wicker basket.

"What have you got there?"

"It's not a sleigh ride without hot chocolate."

"You've thought of everything, haven't you?"

"I've had lots of time." He opened the basket and took out three travel mugs. "This is easier than pouring from a thermos." He offered a mug to Jules, then a kid's sized mug to Becca once he took the reins from her. "You can have these back. I promise."

Jules sipped at her cocoa. "This is delicious. Thank you."

"You're welcome." Dane pulled on the reins. "Whoa, Beau. Whoa, big boy."

Beau stopped.

"Is there a problem?"

Dane smiled. "No. Everything is fine. Look up there." Dane pointed to the night sky above them. "Do you see the stars, Becca? Aren't they something?"

"Wow!"

Dane laughed. "Wow is right!"

"It's breathtaking." Jules marveled at the number of brilliant stars above them. "I've never seen the night sky so bright."

"The sky always looks like this on Christmas Eve." Dane leaned down, his mouth close to Becca's ear. "If you look very carefully, you might even see Santa's sleigh."

Becca gasped. "I will?"

"Yep."

They watched the sky for a moment. "Is that Santa?" Dane pointed at the sky. "Or is that Santa?"

"I don't see him!" Becca said, her voice quivering.

"What was I thinking!" Dane slapped his forehead with his gloved hand. "It's too early for Santa. He's on the other side of the world right now."

"He is?"

"Yes. Do you know what we can do? Look for shooting stars."

They gazed up at the stars. Jules and Dane pointed at shooting stars making their way across the sky. Becca's excitement grew with every shooting star she found.

Jules caught Dane's attention and mouthed the words, "Thank you."

Dane winked in response.

"Did you know that if you make a wish on a shooting star, it will come true?"

"It will?"

"Yes. Go ahead. Try it."

"Close your eyes, sweetheart, and think of something you want," Jules said.

"I did it!"

"Good for you."

"Now you do it, Dane."

Dane closed his eyes. He didn't have to try hard to come up with a wish. He knew what he wanted—to be a family with these two redheads.

"Done. Did Mommy make a wish?"

"Yes, I did."

"Yay! We all made wishes!"

"There's one more thing for us to do," Dane said.

"What's that?" Becca asked.

Dane slipped off his gloves and reached into his coat pocket. He brought out a velvet box.

"Red, no more playing boyfriend-girlfriend. It's time we played for keeps. Will you marry me?"

"Say yes, Mommy!"

"She has to see the ring first, sweetie. She may not like it," Dane teased. "Go on, Jules, open it."

Jules took the small velvet box from him and opened it. She wiped at the tears running down her cheeks. "I ..."

"It belonged to my Grandmother. If you don't like it, I'll buy you another one, whatever you want."

"No! That's not what I was going to say. I didn't expect you to propose."

"You love me, don't you?"

"Yes."

"And I love you. Come on, Red. You know how this goes. I ask you to marry me, and you say yes."

"Say it, Mommy!"

Jules gazed down at Becca. "Before I say yes, I want you to know something, sweetheart. Dane's your daddy."

"He is?"

"Yes, he is."

"Yay!" Becca clapped her mittened hands. "It came true!"

"What came true?"

"My wish. I wished for Dane to be my daddy!"

Dane gazed at Jules. "So? Are you going to make my wish come true?"

"Yes! It's a yes!"

"Yay!" Becca cheered.

Dane leaned over Becca and kissed Jules. It was a soft kiss, one that promised many more to come. "I love you. Now my wish has come true."

Becca snuggled into Dane's side and yawned. "I knew you were my daddy. We have little ears."

Dane laughed. "We sure do, little one. We sure do."

"Someone's ready for bed, and I have a feeling she'll be up bright and early in the morning. Do you mind if we head back, Dane?"

"Home, Beau," Dane called out. "Let's get our girls home."

Beau answered with a whinny then turned to make his way back to the ranch.

Once her stocking hung over the fireplace, a plate of oatmeal cookies and a glass of milk had been left out for Santa, along with carrots for the reindeer, Becca was ready for bed. She kissed everyone good night, including Bates and Lucky. Jules was sure she saw Bates get teary-eyed.

Becca settled into her bed and fell asleep soon after her head touched her pillow.

"Do you think she knew you were her daddy because of your ears?"

"She is smart."

"Too smart if a four-year-old could figure that out."

"Four almost five-year-old," Dane reminded her. "I'm sure it's the almost five that makes her smart." He put his arm around her waist and led her back to the living room.

Val had set out a tray of filled champagne glasses for the four of them.

"In celebration of your engagement, and your first Christmas as a family."

Everyone took a glass and held it out. "Cheers."

"Merry Christmas," Bates added.

"Thank you, Bates. Merry Christmas to you."

They waited for the drinks to finish and Val and Bates to head off to their rooms before Dane and Jules snuggled on the sofa in front of the fire.

"I thought they'd never leave," Dane murmured.

"Don't say that. It's not nice."

"I've been waiting to have you all to myself since you agreed to marry me. I think I've been very patient."

"For a man who has lain in the same spot for several days without moving, I think you weren't even close to being patient."

Dane straightened, turning so that he could gaze into the eyes of the woman who uttered those words. "What did you say?"

"You didn't hear me?"

"I heard you. It's what you said. Red, you joked about me being a sniper."

"You didn't like it?"

"Of course, I liked it! It's just that coming from you, it's unexpected."

"I know. I'm the first to admit that I'd be out the door as soon as I thought about you shooting people. But now. . ." she hesitated.

"Now?"

"I saw first hand how you and Bates saved Val by using a gun without killing John Sinclair. I'd hate to have his ghost haunting that house."

"You're making another joke?"

"No. I'm serious. If that evil man died in my house, I could never set foot in it again."

"You don't have to set foot in it. Your home is here now. Remember?"

Jules held up her ring finger and admired the diamond ring that adorned it. "Do you think your grandmother would have approved of me?"

"Definitely."

"How do you know?"

Dane settled back in the sofa and wrapped his arm around Jules' shoulders. "You are everything she told me to look for in a woman."

"Redheaded, hot-tempered, and opinionated?"

"Someone with a beautiful soul, a smile that brightens my day, and someone who can cook and clean and keep my home spotless."

"She didn't say that!"

"Grandma told me that my heart would know when I found the right woman. I'd feel that ache in my chest when I wasn't with her."

"Did your heart ache for me?"

"It doesn't now. That's all that matters."

"I'm not a homemaker. I have a cleaning lady that comes every week to my house. I don't bake. I can barely cook."

"We'll keep Val with us forever."

"Do you mean that?"

"She's welcome to stay here as long as she wants. Bates, too."

"Bates, too?"

"To use a word our daughter is quite fond of using, yep."

"I'm good with that."

Working together they filled Becca's stocking and one each for Val and Bates. Lucky got a stocking filled with dog snacks. Dane retrieved wrapped presents that had been hidden away in his office then placed them under the tree. When they finished, they stood back and admired the lit Christmas tree with all of its trimming and the presents underneath it.

"You were right." Jules nodded her approval. "The popcorn strings do make it a Christmas tree."

"I think that calls for a celebration of milk and cookies."

Jules looked at the untouched plate of goodies left for Santa. "It's your job. Dads always eat Santa's treats."

Dane shrugged. "Well, they are my favorite and Lucky's." Dane popped a cookie into his mouth and tossed one to Lucky. Lucky gobbled his treat in one bite. Dane took the last cookie and broke it in half, and offered a piece to Jules. "Mrs. Claus?"

Jules took the cookie and bit into it. "Val makes the best cookies." She broke the remainder of her half into small bits and left them on the plate. "Santa always leaves crumbs."

Dane drank most of the glass of milk and placed the glass beside the plate. "We're done."

"Carrots?" Jules pointed to the reindeer's treat.

Dane scooped up the bunch of carrots and carried them to the kitchen where he returned them to the refrigerator's vegetable crisper.

"Ready for bed?" he asked Jules when he returned to the living room.

"Just one more thing to do," Jules answered. Her hands were behind her back.

"What's that?"

She smiled then lifted one hand above her head. Mistletoe. "Give me my Christmas kiss, Gary."

Dane took her in his arms and kissed her. It was a kiss full of longing, one that let her know how much he had missed her. She kissed him back, letting him know that she had missed him, too.

Chapter Sixteen

THEY WALKED TO THEIR BEDROOM holding hands. The click of Lucky's toenails on the wood floor reminded Jules that they weren't alone.

"He'll always be in the bedroom with us?"

"Always. Don't worry love. He'll keep our secrets."

"It's not our secrets that I'm worried about. I've never shared a bedroom with a dog. What if he watches us?"

Dane smiled. "I'm sure he'll have better things to do like dreaming about chasing lions."

Dane opened the door to the master bedroom, then closed it behind them once they were inside. Soft lighting gave off a warm glow. Jules made her way to the bathroom, while Dane sat down on the bed, taking in the view of the room. So much had changed in a few days. His bedroom, decorated for a man, now showed evidence of a woman sharing it with him. The table beside the armchair by the fireplace now had a vase with a fresh Christmas bouquet. The throw blanket and pillows on the sofa displayed Christmas scenes hand-knit by Val. Antique Christmas decorations filled in the empty spaces on the mantle over the fireplace. Most important of all, his bedside table now had a framed photograph of Jules and Becca.

Jules stood in the doorway of the bathroom, watching him. At first, she had wondered if it was too much—adding some of her things to Dane's room. She had returned to her home to pick up a few items for her and Becca, including Becca's Christmas presents, and ended up coming back with a few boxes of Christmas decorations, as well. Dane didn't complain. Instead, he helped her unpack and watched her make herself at home. There was no containing his excitement, knowing that they would be spending Christmas together as a family.

She didn't realize how much family meant to Dane. She cried when he told her that his parents abandoned him when he was a child, and although his grandparents raised him and loved him, he could never forget that feeling of being unwanted and unloved. That was the reason behind his rescue missions—every child needs to know they matter.

He caught her watching him. He didn't know how long she'd been standing there. Jules was ready for bed. Her long hair was now in a messy bun, and she'd changed from jeans and sweater into a tank top and boy shorts. Dane gave Jules an approving nod before making his way to her. She blushed under his gaze, no longer embarrassed by her reaction to him.

"Where'd you go? Is everything all right?"

"Just thinking about this room's new decorating. Something's missing."

"Oh? What's that?"

"You, naked in my bed." In one swift move, Dane picked Jules up and carried her caveman style over his shoulder to his bed.

Jules laughed. "What's gotten into you?"

Dane let her down gently onto the bed. "Arms up."

She obeyed, lifting her arms for Dane to pull off her top.

"Shorts." Jules lifted her hips, allowing Dane to pull the underwear off her.

"You're still dressed. No fair."

Dane grabbed the hem of his shirt and pulled it over his head, dropping it to the floor. Within seconds his pants and underwear were on the floor. "Fast enough for you?" He then joined her, lying on his side to face her.

His expression became serious. "You're the most beautiful woman I have ever known, and I can't believe how lucky I am to have you in my life."

"It goes both ways. If you hadn't been in your bar that night, we wouldn't be here. Our Becca wouldn't be here." Jules reached for Dane and clasped her hands around his neck. "I have a confession to make. I haven't been with anyone since our night together. I may be a bit rusty at this."

Dane kissed her softly on the lips. "Focus on us. Let yourself go. I know you can do it."

"What if your memories of me are overrated?"

"What about me? What if I'm not up to your expectations? Besides, I'm the one with the head injury."

"Don't joke about that."

"Jules, we'll be fine. We love each other. That's all that matters." His hand tilted her chin up, bringing her mouth closer to his. "All we need is that kiss. You know the one, the one that curls your toes."

Jules gasped. "She told you?"

"I heard you tell Doc. Be careful what you say when you think I'm out cold, love. I still hear you." For a moment, he gazed at her. He adored her mouth. No matter what barbs she threw at him, he could never take his eyes off the fullness of her lips. Then he kissed her and tasted champagne mixed with her unique flavor that reminded him of spicy cinnamon. A soft moan escaped from him when she accepted his kiss and opened her mouth to him, tasting him.

Jules felt her body melting into his. She ached for more, memories of his touch rousing her body from a five years' long hibernation. "More," she gasped against his lips. "I need more."

Dane answered her with a lusty smile. His brown eyes had changed, darkened by the raw emotions flowing through him. He had never been aroused by a woman the way that Red affected him. Their one night together had branded him, forever marking his heart claimed by the redheaded beauty. "You don't know how much I've missed you."

"Show me, Gary. Show me."

Dane's fingers traced slowly over Jules' alabaster skin from her shoulder down to the curve of her hip, then made their way back up her body. Her skin tingled under his touch. His mouth joined his fingers in rediscovering Red's body. He remembered everything about her. The taste and smell of her filled his senses. Dane took a nipple into his mouth, sucking on the rosy bud then flicked it with his tongue until it stood erect.

"Dane."

"Hmm," he murmured.

"I need you inside me. Please. We can have foreplay later."

He released her nipple from his mouth and gazed into her eyes. "It won't be foreplay then. Unless we make love again."

Jules moved to her back, giving him complete access to her. She wanted him between her legs. She needed to have him inside her, filling the emptiness she had felt the moment she had left his bed what felt like a lifetime ago.

"Don't play games with me. Just do it."

"Hold on." He moved to get off the bed.

"What?"

"I have to get a condom. It may not be from Las Vegas and covered in glitter, but I can almost guarantee it won't break." He hadn't forgotten when they first slept together. He didn't have a condom to use, and all Red could offer was a souvenir condom from a girls' weekend in Las Vegas. The glitter from the package seemed to land everywhere. For months afterward, Dane would find glitter throughout his condo. The condom also broke.

"I don't want you to use one."

"Mind telling me why?" He settled back onto the bed.

Jules relaxed under his gaze. "I don't know if I can get pregnant again. The odds of conceiving Becca were almost nonexistent."

"If we did conceive again, how would you feel?"

"Like the luckiest woman in the world."

"That's all I needed to hear."

Dane moved onto Jules, careful to support his weight with his arms. Her legs opened to him, instantly wrapping around his waist. He entered her slowly, giving her body time to adjust to him. Jules rolled her hips under his weight, rubbing against his shaft.

"You're going to make me come if you keep that up."

"I don't care. It feels good."

"Let's do this together, love. Take our time."

"I've waited too long for you, Gary. You can have me your way next time."

"Playing by your rules, are we?"

"This time."

Dane bent down to her, his lips soft against her ear, his voice gruff with desire. "Is this what you want, Red?" His thrusts were hard and deep.

"Yes." Jules reached for his hair and pulled. His groan fueled her fire. "More." She held on tight with her legs, pulling him into her. Intense pleasure coursed through her body. Toe-curling pleasure.

"Let yourself go, love. I'll catch you."

Jules cried out her release and heard the rough groan of Dane's orgasm in her ear. She felt herself floating, only to realize it was Dane pulling her onto him. Jules nestled into Dane's firm and sweaty chest and listened to his racing heart while his arms held her to him.

"Is that what you wanted?"

Jules answered with a nod of her head. "What about you?"

Dane kissed the top of her head. "Perfect. I couldn't have wished for more."

Chapter Seventeen

"HE'S GOING TO BE FINE, JULES. We've removed the tumor, and the test confirms that it's benign. He's going to be okay."

Jules squeezed Doc Burns' hand. "Thank you. That's great news. What about Dane's seizures? Do you think the tumor caused them?"

"We don't know for sure. Only time will tell. You can go in and sit with him if you'd like. He's going to be out for quite a while. Or go home, and we'll call you when he wakes up."

"I'll stay. I promised Becca I would stay with Dane since he doesn't have Lucky to protect him."

Doc Burns smiled. "That damned dog. Best thing I ever did for that man was insisting that he get that dog."

"My aunt calls him Dane's lifesaver."

"That's true, and Dane saved Lucky's life, too. He's a rescue dog."

"I didn't know that."

"Yes. Fortunately for Lucky, he was spotted by a woman who trains service dogs. There was something about him that made her think he could do the job."

"He does it quite well."

"Yes, he does."

Jules thanked Doc Burns then left to sit by Dane's bedside. As a doctor, she was used to the monitors and intravenous lines. Jules reached for Dane's hand. It was cold—nothing to cause alarm. As Dane's lover, she wanted him to feel warm. Spotting a blanket on the empty bed next to his, Jules retrieved the blanket and covered Dane.

She sat down again and took Dane's hand in hers. She felt conflicted, knowing the importance of recovery time, and yet impatient for Dane to awaken. Jules wanted to hear his voice, to hear that he was fine. She wanted him to open his eyes and give her that boyish wink she'd become used to and found sexy as sin. Dane had told her that he could hear her when he was coming out of a seizure. Although this wasn't the same, it wouldn't hurt to start talking to him.

"Dane, can you hear me? It's Jules. You're out of surgery. The tumor's gone. You're going to be fine. Everything's going to be fine."

Jules waited for a response. When none came, she continued their one-sided conversation.

"You're still not out of the doghouse, mister. As Becca's parents, we are supposed to discuss and agree on what presents we give our child. I know that we aren't married. But still, giving Becca a puppy for Christmas and a pony! You don't have to give a child everything she has on her wish list all in one day." Jules sighed then smiled. "Although I have to admit that they are two of the cutest animals I have ever seen. Popsy's adorable. Her ears are so long that she's tripping over them. Now that she's got the paper training mastered, Val won't give me grief over her peeing on the floor. Why she won't tell you off, I don't know. It's not because you're her boss. I've heard her tell you off when you deserved it. I wonder if it's because of your tumor. . .well, if she was taking pity on you, those days are over. No one pities my man."

Jules straightened, feeling the heat in her cheeks. "Look at me. I'm getting mad over nothing." She sighed. "It's true. I am a hot-headed redhead. Heaven help us if Becca has my temper. We've been lucky. She's perfect. She gets that from you."

She got to her feet and made her way to the window. The view it offered was of the blue, grey and white of the mountains. "I didn't realize how much I'd missed the Rockies until I returned home. Maybe if you can ride again, we can take Becca with us and go on a trail ride. I'd love to do that. I've heard terrible things about how ornery ponies can be. You'll have to convince me that Peanuts won't hurt our girl. You're probably a pony whisperer just like you are with dogs and horses."

Jules returned to her chair. Taking hold of Dane's hand, she brought it to her lips and kissed it. "You have the biggest heart of anyone I know. I love you, Dane Andrews."

"My name's Gary," his voice croaked. The words stuck to his tongue. His mouth dry from the anesthetic.

Jules offered Dane a glass of water. "Here, take a sip."

Dane raised his head from the pillow, sipped from the straw, then let his head fall back onto the pillow. He closed his eyes.

"Sometimes, I call you Gary, but your name is Dane. Can you tell me where you are?"

"I'm in the hospital. With you. Red. Gary."

"Yes, that's true. But tell me your real name and mine. Please do that for me."

"Let me go back to sleep. I'm tired."

"Dane, wake up. Please. You can do it."

"Red."

"I'm here."

"There's something you should know."

Jules felt a tightness in her chest. "What is it?"

"The ring. Your ring. Do you have it?"

"Yes, I have it on. I've never taken it off."

"Read the inscription."

"Why?"

"Just read it. Please."

Jules slipped the ring off her finger, and read aloud the inscription engraved on the inside, "To Margaret Gary. Yours forever, Daniel."

"Your grandmother's name was Gary?"

Dane nodded. "My middle name, too."

"So all this time—"

"I've always been your Gary."

Chapter Eighteen

They decided on a February wedding. Valentine's Day to be exact. Although many thought the couple had chosen this day because of it being one of the most romantic days of the year, Jules and Dane knew the truth. Valentine's Day was the day of Gary and Red's first make believe date. It would be too hard to explain, and no one needed to know the games Dane and Jules liked to play as Gary and Red. Only Lucky, and he didn't tell a soul.

Jules stood in the master bedroom, gazing at her reflection in the dressing mirror.

"You're the most beautiful bride I've ever seen," Val gushed as she dabbed at her tears. "I wish your Mom and Dad were here to see you today."

Jules hugged her aunt. "I do, too. I've got you, and you mean the world to me. I know I haven't been the easiest to live with, and yet you've always been there for me."

"When you were a teenager, there were times when Ned and I wondered if we'd survive you, and then we'd think of your mother, and we knew we'd make it work." Val stepped back from her niece. "I have something for you. It was your mother's. She asked me to give it to you on your wedding day."

Val opened her clutch purse and took out a green velvet bag. She offered it to Jules. Jules took the bag and looked at Val.

"Open it, sweetheart."

Jules loosened the satin strings of the bag. She gasped when she looked at its contents.

"Your father gave her the pearl necklace on their wedding day. He gave her the earrings on the day you were born."

Jules struggled with the clasp. "Will you help me put them on? My hands are shaking."

"Of course." Val took the necklace and stood behind Jules, placing the pearls around her neck and fastening the clasp. Her nimble fingers then put each perfect pearl drop in Jules' ears.

"How do I look?"

Val stood beside Jules and joined her in admiring the reflection of the beautiful bride. Jules wore a modest mermaid wedding dress in white with long lace sleeves that tapered up to the elbow from her wrist. The scalloped neckline was the perfect frame for the single strand of pearls. The dress fit perfectly, showing off her feminine curves. Jules wore her hair long, her red hair falling in thick waves to her shoulders, the way Dane liked it. It was the only request he made of his bride to be.

"You are stunning."

"And so are you, Aunt Val. I wish Uncle Ned could see you." Val wore a soft mauve brocade dress with a chiffon jacket. It was a perfect match with her silver hair.

A light rap at the bedroom door interrupted them.

"Come in," Jules called out.

Doc Burns opened the door peering around it before opening the door fully. "I have a little girl here who wants to see her mommy."

"It's all right. I'm ready."

Doc Burns opened the door wide, and Becca came running into the room. She wore a floor-length white lace dress that matched the lace in Jules' sleeves. In her hair, she had a white bow that matched the bow at her waist.

"Mommy," she called out excitedly. "You're beautiful!"

Jules kneeled and embraced her daughter. "You're beautiful, too, sweetheart. Are you ready to go see Daddy?"

Becca nodded her head. "Let's get married!"

Dane waited patiently in front of the living room's fireplace with Bates by his side and Lucky at his feet. The men looked sharp in their black tuxedos and black ties. Lucky wore a matching bow tie on his collar.

"I've got your six," Bates said. "In case you change your mind."

Dane smiled. "Not a chance, my friend. Thanks for the offer, though."

Val had not left out one detail when decorating the living room for the wedding ceremony. Furniture had been rearranged to accommodate the small number of guests. Candles and winter greenery gave the room a romantic charm, as did the vases filled with pink, burgundy, and white flowers. Nothing was out of place. Chairs arranged in a semi-circle faced the fireplace.

There were only a few close friends who Dane and Jules wanted to share in their special day. Dane invited the men and women who worked with him. They were his extended family, all of whom would risk their lives for Dane and everyone else in their small group. Mark Blackwell and his partner were in attendance.

"I think we're ready," the minister said when he spotted Val standing in the hallway giving him the nod. "Ladies and gentlemen, if you would please rise for the bride."

He smiled when Becca made her appearance carrying her bouquet. Her face was one big toothy smile as she walked down the short aisle. Val followed behind her, dabbing at tears. They took their places across from Dane.

An audible gasp greeted Jules when she made her appearance. She walked down the aisle with her head held high. Her emerald eyes sparkled. Dane could see them from where he stood. His gaze didn't leave her, taking in her beauty while marveling that this woman was soon to be his wife. Dane held out his hand to her, and she accepted it. She stepped closer to him, and he greeted her with a soft kiss. Jules felt the blush come to her face.

"You're beautiful," Dane said softly.

Jules looked deep into his brown eyes and felt herself melting into them. She could see the love he felt for her, and she knew that he could see the same love for him reflected in her eyes.

The minister smiled at the couple. "Shall we begin?"

They said their vows and exchanged rings. Their eyes never looked at anything or anyone but each other. When the minister proclaimed them husband and wife, the guests gave a loud cheer. Dane took Jules into his arms and kissed her until they were both breathless.

When he released her, Dane scooped Becca into his arm and hugged her and Jules close to his chest. "You and Becca have made me the happiest man alive. I couldn't wish for more."

"How about one more, in about eight months?"

"Are you sure?" Dane felt his heart was about to burst out of his chest.

"Yes, I'm sure."

"What do you think about that, Becca? Mommy's going to give you a baby brother or sister!"

"Yay! My wish came true."

"All of our wishes have come true, sweetheart. And more."

Book Club Questions

How did the book make you feel?

- Were you amused, bored, intrigued by Dane and Jules' story?
- Are you glad you read it?

What did you think about the main characters?

- Were they believable?
- Which character did you relate to the most/least?
- Was Dane's medical condition believable?
- Was Jules' reaction to guns/snipers authentic?
- Was Dane's occupation something you find interesting or admire?
- Was Jules' hot headedness too much?
- If you were to be one of the characters, who would you be? Why?

Which parts of the book stood out to you?

- Are there quotes, passages, or scenes that you found particularly compelling?
- Were there scenes that you thought were unique, out of place, thought-provoking or disturbing?
- Could you see yourself in any of the situations?

What themes did you detect in the story?

- Have you ever been in a situation where you needed someone to save you?

- Have you ever had to step in and help someone out of a bad situation?
- Have you ever had to overlook or accept something so that you could have a relationship with someone?

Knowing that Dane owned the bar, should he have thrown John Sinclair out right away?

- Do you think that Jules was in danger at any time?

What do you think motivated Jules to stay in the bar with Sinclair lurking in the background?

- Did you feel fearful for her?

Why do you think that Jules needed a man to step in versus dealing with Sinclair herself?

- Do you think Dane was playing a mind game by letting him stay?
- The name of the bar is The Admiral's Eighth. Do you know what the term means?
- Would you approach a stranger in a bar for help? Have you ever had to ask a stranger for help?

What do you think of Bates?

- Do you know anyone like him?
- Would you like to read his story?

Did the ending pull you in? Did you want more?

- Were you satisfied or disappointed with how it ended?
- How do you picture the characters' lives after the end of the story?
- If you were to identify the most important theme within Boss, what would it be?

What changes/decisions would you hope for if the story were made into a movie?

- Which sections would you cut?
- Who would you cast to play the main characters?

How does *Boss* compare to other romance novels you've read?

- Do you want to read more in the series?

What is your impression of the author?

- What do you think of the author's writing style?
- What do you think of the author's storytelling ability?
- Would you read another book by the same author?

Please enjoy the
opening chapter of

Bates

the next book in the series

Chapter One

Jon Bates cursed the day that a cup of coffee became more than what it was—a black consumable liquid made by pouring boiling water over ground coffee beans. Lattes, cappuccinos, and mochaccinos? What the hell was that shit? He shifted his weight while standing in line to place his order. He had things to do, and standing in this line listening to people trying to make up their minds as to what to order was getting on his nerves.

"Next! May I take your order?"

Jon stepped forward. "You're not Marge." He glanced at her name tag. *Pam.*

"Thanks for noticing. Marge has moved to another location closer to home. You've got me now. What can I get for you?" She gave him her best smile.

"Two large coffees. Black."

"Anything to eat with it? We have banana-walnut muffins just out of the oven."

"No. Just coffee."

"Ok, maybe next time. What name do you want on your cup?"

His eyebrows arched. "Excuse me?"

"Your name. So we can give you your coffee. No screw-ups."

"Can't you just pour it now and give it to me?"

"Sorry, it doesn't work that way. We have a protocol we have to follow."

Jon looked behind him, noticing the impatience in the woman standing behind him.

He turned his attention back to the server. "Jon. No h."

"Thank you. You can get your order over there." The server pointed to the end of the counter.

"Fucking unbelievable," he muttered under his breath.

"I heard that, John No H."

He glanced at her to find her smiling at him while she took another customer's order.

"They should have a line for coffee only, and the other line for the other caffeinated or non-caffeinated shit. We'd get our coffee a lot faster."

Jon turned his attention to the woman who had voiced his exact thoughts. "Damned straight." She was petite with blonde hair and blue eyes. Her cheeks still held the pink from the outside winter's cold. Her heavy winter coat hid the rest of her from him.

"Then again," she offered, "we wouldn't get the chance to talk to another human being while we waited for our coffee. Look at them." She nodded to the other patrons standing in line, their gaze focused on their cellphone screens. "They're more concerned with what's out there than who's in here."

"John No H!"

Jon nodded his head and reached for the offered tray holding two large coffee cups.

"Have a great day, Jon No H," the petite blonde said to him as he turned to leave.

"Thanks. You, too."

• • •

He drove slowly along the cemetery's driveway. The dead deserved respect, especially the fallen soldiers. Bates stopped his black SUV when he caught up with Dane Andrews, the man he called Boss. Boss was his best friend, his naval buddy, his lifesaver. Bates turned off the ignition and exited the vehicle, taking the tray with coffee cups with him.

Boss's service dog acknowledged Bates' arrival with a glance before focusing his attention back on his master.

Boss took the offered coffee. "Thanks." He raised the cup as if toasting the headstone he stood beside. "Here's to you, Mikey. You were a damned good Navy man. Gone too soon."

"Second that," Bates said.

Both men took a sip from their cups then poured a small amount over the gravesite.

"Damn, that man loved his coffee."

"It's all he lived on near the end."

"Too bad it couldn't save him." Boss looked at Bates with serious eyes. "If you ever consider taking yourself out of the game, you talk to me first. Do you hear me, Corporal?"

"Yes, Sir."

"I swear that I will follow you into the bowels of Hell and beat the shit out of you if you do."

Bates smiled. "What makes you think I'd go to Hell?"

"Don't suicides go to Hell?"

"Only if you believe in it, and I believe that there's enough of Hell on earth that we don't need it anywhere else."

"Amen to that." Boss took another drink from his coffee cup before he emptied the contents onto the grave. "Sleep well, my friend. Sleep well."

Bates did the same, drinking from his cup before pouring the rest of it onto the gravesite. It was then that Boss noticed the writing on his coffee cup.

"John No H?"

"Don't ask."

"Bates would have been easier."

"There's nothing hard about spelling Jon the right way."

"Apparently there is." Boss chuckled as they made there way back to the SUV. "You dropped Val off at Jules'?"

"Where else would I have taken her?"

"Just checking."

"The woman doesn't know how to clean off her walkway. Someone could get hurt."

"I'm sure you took care of it. Thanks."

Dane liked to tease Bates, knowing that he was a stickler to detail. He never went off course, always did what was expected of him. He made sure that everyone around him was safe, or as safe as possible, especially when it came to Jules, Becca, the child he fathered with Jules, and Val, his housekeeper and Jules' aunt.

Bates' cellphone rang. He answered it on the first ring, putting it on speakerphone. "Hello?"

"Bates, we can't find Becca. Please come and help us."

Dane and his service dog started to run to the SUV before Bates answered Val.

"What the hell happened?" Dane demanded as they both reached the SUV and jumped in.

"Damned if I know, but we'll find out soon enough," Bates answered as he sped out of the cemetery. Respect for the dead was the last thing on his mind.

About the Author

Deborah Armstrong hit the big 50, and became restless and couldn't concentrate on much. Her favourite escape was to read. Instantly, her daughter's romance novels became the ultimate magnet. Hours were spent devouring them.

That was then...this is now. Deborah turned her restlessness into writing hot and spicy contemporary romance with a touch of country. She attributes her love of the English language, reading and writing to her parents. She is thrilled to have passed on her love of books (with the help of her husband, also an avid reader) to her children and grandchildren.

Deborah lives with her husband and five hundred cows on their dairy farm in Ontario, Canada. When she's not writing or working on the farm, she enjoys reading, travelling watching movies and spending time with her family and friends. Her writing muse tends to run on the liquid side: strong coffee, chocolate milk and single malt scotch in no particular order.

Thrice each week, the local gym beckons. Cardio means book thinking time for unravelling plots and conversations for her current work in progress.

When Deborah's characters talk, she listens. Not surprisingly, they decide when and how to tell their story, talking to her at the strangest times. When she's driving, working out or trying to fall asleep, they whisper in her ear and say, "This is what needs to happen next."

Stay connected with Deborah

Deborah Armstrong is a storyteller, creating fantasies and weaving them for your reading delight from her farm in Caledon, Canada.

If you are in a Book Club, bring Deborah to yours via Skype...or in person! Whether it's a hot and steamy summer day or one kissed with a wintery landscape, have your Club gather their favourite snacks and beverages and discover Boss.

Deborah invites her readers to follow her on social media and to contact her by email. To work with her, visit her website and subscribe to her newsletter.

Deborah@DeborahArmstrong.ca

www.DeborahArmstrong.ca

Facebook

Pinterest

Instagram

Twitter